The
Legally Binding
Christmas:
A Courtroom Adventure

D1417491

Always Believe !
Julis

The Legally Binding Christmas: A Courtroom Adventure
Copyright © 2016 by Landis Wade
(Hamlin Landis Wade, Jr.)
www.landiswade.com
All rights reserved.

Trade 978-0-9974484-5-0
eBook 978-0-9974484-6-7

Library of Congress Control Number: 2016947483
Fiction-Fantasy General

This is a work of fiction. The characters, incidents and dialogue come from the writer's imagination and any similarities to actual persons or events is coincidental. Please honor the writer and illustrator. Except for brief excerpts for reviews, no portion of the text and no illustrations may be reproduced without written permission from the writer.

Address your requests to landiswrites@gmail.com or to the publisher at the address given below.

Cover and interior illustrations by
Susanne Discenza Frueh, sfrueh@gmail.com

Book design by Frogtown Bookmaker
frogtownbookmaker.com

Published by Lystra Books & Literary Services, LLC
391 Lystra Estates Drive, Chapel Hill, NC 27517
919-968-7877

lystrabooks@gmail.com
www.lystrabooks.com

Printed in the United States of America

LYSTRA BOOKS
& Literary Services

Praise for *The Legally Binding Christmas*

Well, would you look at that. It warms my heart to see an attorney burning the midnight oil on a creative endeavor, of all things, and this story will surely warm the hearts of readers. If you don't feel like watching *It's a Wonderful Life* for a third time this holiday season, mix things up a bit and read this sweet Christmas story instead.

- Mary Laura Philpott, co-author of
Poetic Justice: Legal Humor in Verse

In *The Legally Binding Christmas*, lawyer Landis Wade continues the good fight to save Christmas for True Believers in a riveting courtroom drama. Defense attorney Thad Raker returns to battle a high-powered opponent intent on using eminent domain to take a humble-looking property that, as it turns out, is critical to the very spirit of Christmas. Along the way, his own faith in the season and himself is restored. A heart-warming story for all ages.

- Charles Blackburn, Jr.,
author of *Sweet Souls and Other Stories*

Landis Wade once again proves that the combination of Christmas cheer and courtroom drama makes for an irresistible read. Only a lawyer at home in the courtroom could have conjured the intrigue of the jury trial that appears here. From judge to opposing attorney to the client who listens—but only partly—to his lawyer, Wade deftly weaves together large amounts of verisimilitude with a good bit of Christmas magic. The result is a rollicking story that serves justice up on a colorful Christmas platter.

- Maxine Eichner,
Graham Kenan Professor of Law, UNC Law School

If you don't believe in Santa when you start this book, then you will when you finish. A perfect complement to *The Christmas Heist*, with just the right mix of suspense, humor and magic, this book will be equally enjoyable to teenagers and adults alike. I love it!

- Bud Schill, co-author of
Not Exactly Rocket Scientists and Other Stories

Landis Wade brings to life the genuine and true magic of Christmas in a classic legal battle. Attorney extraordinaire Thad Raker again accepts the challenge of protecting Christmas, as well as an unusual client who is about to lose his property to the government. The courtroom duel pitches Raker against a well-funded, pompous opponent. The outcome will warm your heart and *The Legally Binding Christmas* will be an instant seasonal favorite.

- Tommy Odom,
North Carolina Eminent Domain Trial Attorney

Landis Wade has employed his considerable legal skills to wrap a fanciful Christmas tale in the package of a hotly contested eminent domain lawsuit. An interesting array of trial participants, matched with numerous literary comparisons such as the landowner's opposing pompous counsel, who "would blow like a whale in distress," keeps one's attention as the trial proceeds until the marvelous verdict is pronounced.

Wade convinces us that to once again achieve True Believer status is a worthy goal.

- Forrest A. Ferrell,
Superior Court Judge, retired

To *The Christmas Heist* readers,
whose kind words
led me to write another.

Also by Landis Wade

The Christmas Heist: A Courtroom Adventure

Visit the author's website,
www.landiswade.com

Visit the Facebook page
www.facebook.com/thechristmasheist

THE LEGALLY BINDING CHRISTMAS:

A Courtroom Adventure

by

Landis Wade

LYSTRA BOOKS
& Literary Services

Chapel Hill, NC

To the top of the porch! to the top of the wall!
Now dash away! dash away! dash away all!

'Twas The Night Before Christmas

Seven Years Earlier – Summertime

5:55 p.m.

The twelve jurors shuffled into the courtroom and down the two rows of seats they had occupied for the past three days. They sat down and looked straight ahead. Attorney Thad Raker took notice; they weren't looking at him, or at his client. It was not a good sign.

"Has the jury reached a verdict?" the judge asked.

The foreman stood. "Yes, sir. We have."

"Hand it to the bailiff, please."

The bailiff accepted the slip of paper and walked it over to the judge, who read it, handed it to the clerk and nodded for her to proceed.

The clerk asked the jury to stand and acknowledge the verdict. "In the case of Roscoe Ledbetter versus Gloria Patten, you answered the issues on the verdict sheet as follows:

"Issue 1: Did Gloria Patten negligently lose control of her motor vehicle and cause damage to Roscoe Ledbetter's personal property?

"Answer: Yes.

"Issue 2: Was Gloria Patten's conduct in the operation of her motor vehicle excused by a sudden emergency?

"Answer: No.

"Issue 3: How much, if any, does Gloria Patten owe Roscoe Ledbetter for the damage she caused?

"Answer: $75,000.

"Is this your verdict, so say you all?"

The jurors responded in the affirmative. The judge dismissed them. And the case was over. Just like that.

Raker realized Gloria Patten was in a tough spot. She was 62 years old and didn't have $75,000 to pay the plaintiff, much less to pay him, and the court would sell what was left of her damaged car and most of her personal belongings to pay the judgment; she would be left with no assets, an apartment she couldn't afford and no place to go. And for what? Three dead cows, some damaged farm equipment and a spoiled winter crop. She would suffer because of the way he tried the case.

Gloria interrupted his thoughts with a hand on his arm. "It's not your fault, Thad. You told me to tell the truth. And I did. It was the right thing to do."

Raker looked at her and thought of his late grandmother, who was too sweet to lay blame even where blame was due. It was his job to advise his client about strategy, and he had failed, because the jurors had spoken; none of them believed her story. Ms. Patten's truth was nothing more than the product of her vivid imagination.

As he left the courtroom, Raker heard several lawyers joking about the trial. Raker knew he deserved it. He had based the defense on the magic of Christmas. It was no way to win a case.

On the drive home, he was discouraged. Depressed, more like it. He wondered what would become of Gloria Patten. The future of his own career was another question, but he chided himself for giving it a thought when he'd let his client down.

A sad song played on the radio as he pulled into the driveway of his modest two-bedroom house. His sister, Laura, greeted him at the door with a beverage.

"I think you need this, little brother," she said.

"Thanks. Sorry I'm so late. The jury didn't come back until around 6:00."

"Not to worry, Thad. You know you can count on me."

All his life, Raker's big sister had been his lifeline, but even more so in the last four years. Without her help, Raker knew it would have been impossible to carry on after his wife's funeral.

Just then, a little ball of fire in the form of a 4-year-old girl with a head full of blond curls ran into the room. "Daddy, you're home!" She wrapped her arms around his knees.

"There's my girl." Raker bent down to give her a kiss on the head. "How was your day?"

"It was so much fun, Daddy. Aunt Laura took me to lunch and then we came home and took Comet for a walk." As an afterthought, she said, "They don't let dogs eat at restaurants."

Comet must have heard his name because he charged into the room and joined the welcome. Raker rubbed his head. "Hey, pup. How ya doin'?"

Comet replied with a wagging tale; he had an excited look on his face. The dog was a mutt, no ifs, ands or buts. Raker discovered him as a puppy wandering the streets on Christmas Eve, one month after Liz was born. He shot out of nowhere and into Raker's heart when he needed him most. Raker brought him home, fed him and made him part of the family.

"Oh, and Daddy, we saw Ms. Sarah today. She said to say hi."

Raker looked at his sister for an answer.

"At lunch," Laura said. "Sarah wanted to catch up with me and see Liz, so we went to a restaurant near her office. She asked how you are doing."

"She will know when she reads the morning paper."

"Thad, even though she's a lawyer, I doubt she cares only about your cases."

Raker thought about Sarah Kennedy and felt uncomfortable. Sarah was Laura's best friend and had spent time at his house visiting with Laura while she cared for Liz. She was kind to his little girl and even took her on outings from time to time, but when he thought about Sarah as a woman, he forced himself to think of her only as a friend and colleague. It was too soon to think about another woman in his life.

"Can we play, Daddy?" Liz took his hand and he remembered, despite everything else, that his life still had light in it.

"Tell you what," Raker said. "You brush your teeth, get in bed and I will read you a story. Be there in 10 minutes."

After Liz ran off and Comet followed, Laura gave her brother a hug. "Hard day?" she asked.

"All days are hard days, Sis." He hugged her back. "Shouldn't it be getting less painful by now?"

"That's difficult for me to say. I haven't been in your shoes. It might get harder."

"Harder?"

"Liz is 4 years old and growing up fast. She will remind you of Elizabeth more and more as the years go on. And she will start to understand and see the sadness that haunts you and this house every day. Have you thought about that?"

"Yes, I have. I know I'm sad. I just don't know how to fix it. And I know I need to do better, for Liz's sake." Raker paused. "I'll go read to her; it's as much for me as it is for her."

Laura hugged her brother again. "I love you, Thad. See you at 8:00 tomorrow morning. Oh, and I can't stay late tomorrow night. Can you be home by 5:30?"

"Is this another date with the soon-to-be Mr. Right?" Raker asked.

"Another date, yes, but I know your jury is still out on whether he's the right one," Laura said.

"It's just because you deserve the best," Raker said. "I'll be home in time."

Raker found his daughter sitting up in bed, the covers pulled to her waist. Comet was curled at the end of her bed and he looked up, ready to listen, too. "So what will it be tonight?" Raker went to the bookshelf.

"Not a book, Daddy. Tell me the story again!"

Raker had the anxious feeling he got in his chest every time Liz asked him to tell the story. It took him back to a happy time, but the memories were hard on him; he felt incomplete, a hole in his heart. "But you've heard the story more times than you can count."

She pleaded again, with her smile mostly, and when that didn't work, she said, "Oh, please, Daddy, just one more time!"

Raker sat down on the bed and squeezed her tight. "You are such a little mess."

"Daddy," she whispered, both arms around his neck. "I know I'm a little mess, but tell me the story again. Tell me how I got my name."

Raker reached over and turned out the bedside lamp, leaving only the soft glow from Liz's Mickey Mouse night light. Then, as he did every time he told the story, Raker lay down beside her, put his arm around her and took a deep breath to settle his nerves.

"Elizabeth Henry Raker, you were named after two very special people. One was a brave man named Henry Edmonds, who, at great risk to his freedom, went on trial five years ago to save Christmas and then, for some unknown reason, vanished. The other was your mother, Elizabeth, who gave birth to you four years ago and ..." This was the hardest part, acknowledging out loud that Elizabeth was gone, and trying to explain it to his little girl. It never got easier, but he did it because he wanted Liz to feel pride in the mother she never knew.

"Henry taught me to believe again, just as I did when I was a child. But your mother always believed. She believed in the goodness of people, in hope, in charity, but most of all, she found a way to believe in me even when I didn't believe in myself." As he had done countless times before, Raker ended the story with tears in his eyes. "They would have loved you very much."

Raker stood up and began to tuck Liz in, nice and tight.

She stopped him. "Wait. You left out the part about my nickname."

"You know how you got your nickname."

"I know, but tell it."

"We blame your nickname on Comet. His vocabulary is limited to one-syllable words. I wanted to stick with Elizabeth, but he talked me out of it. We settled on Liz." Comet wagged his tail.

Liz giggled. "Comet can't talk."

"Tell that to Comet. Good night, Liz."

"Good night, Daddy. I love you."

"Love you more."

Present Day – November

8:30 a.m.

Thad Raker was in his law office looking through a window obscured by dense morning fog; he was waiting for a potential client to arrive. The weather fit his mood. It was Liz's 11th birthday. She didn't ask him to tell her bedtime stories anymore, not even the one about how she got her name. He missed that little girl.

He had raised her as a single dad, with the help and tough love of Laura, who now had a husband and two children of her own. She continued to make

sure he rose to the best challenge life could offer —
being Liz's dad.

As Raker's mood began to lift, so did the fog; his
view now revealed the first floor of the county
courthouse across the street. His mind wandered to
the cases he had argued there over the years.

His most famous case was the criminal trial of
Henry Edmonds that had started two days before
Christmas, almost 12 years earlier. The newspaper
reporter covering the case had called it the "trial of
the century." To Raker, it was the trial that changed
his life in more ways than one. It made him a True
Believer, and gave him the courage to ask Elizabeth
to marry him. They were married two weeks later.

Raker came back from his reverie when a voice
called from the office foyer. "Anybody home?"

Raker put on his jacket and walked to meet the
person behind the voice. He found an elderly man,
about 5 feet 10 inches tall, with fine gray hair pulled
around his ears and tied in a tight ponytail. He wore
black slacks, a blue shirt and a red vest under a tweed
jacket. His face was full, with bushy brows and a
prominent nose; it was a cheerful mug, with laugh
lines like lightning strikes on either side of his
mouth. He smiled when he saw Raker. There was
something about the man that Raker liked right away.

"You must be Mr. Masters." Raker held out his hand.

"The name is T. W. Masters, but everyone calls me Twirly. Don't know why. They just do. Guess it's because my parents gave me the nickname. Yep, that must be why they do it. On the other hand, maybe they do it because I talk a lot and it sounds like I'm going in circles. Or maybe they do it because when I was a child I took a ride in a helicopter. What a ride. Do you like to ride in helicopters? No? Anyway, Twirly's my name. Yours is Thad Raker, right?"

As the man talked, Raker sensed the meeting was going to be a waste of time. But he did the courteous thing, inviting Masters into his office and offering him a seat. Raker took the chair behind his desk.

"Should we get the reindeer test out of the way?" Masters asked.

Raker was surprised. How did Twirly Masters know about the reindeer test? Raker developed the test because of the notoriety that followed the "trial of the century." During the first six months after the trial, Raker received at least two calls a week from people who claimed to have some connection to Santa Claus. Most of them were criminal defendants calling from the jail. They wanted the lawyer who got the guy off by proving he worked for Santa Claus. Any lawyer who could do that was the lawyer for them. That's why Raker came up with the test.

"Name the eight reindeer," he would say. The most interesting lies Raker heard in his career came from potential clients who had taken the reindeer test. He remembered one guy who, without hesitation, used the last names of the top eight players from his fantasy football team. Another guy named seven planets and Rudolph. Another tried vegetables. Among them were kale, butterbean and turnip. One finished up with the names of presidents: "On Washington, on Lincoln, on Kennedy and Reagan."

For the first four years, Raker agreed to represent anyone who passed the reindeer test, partly because they sounded sincere and partly because Raker wanted to believe in their stories. But he finally had to admit that he was being too gullible. When he discovered that the clients who passed the test were either frauds or needed psychiatric help, he politely withdrew from their cases. Only once did the blinders stay on too long. It was the Patten case, and like the "trial of the century," it made the news.

"How about it?" Twirly Masters broke into Raker's thoughts again, "Do you want me to take the reindeer test? It's not a problem. Matter of fact, I can do it in reverse."

"Excuse me?"

"Know them so well, I can do it backward."

"That won't be necessary."

"Don't mind a bit. On Blitzen, on Donner, on Cupid and Comet. Now Vixen, now Prancer, now Dancer, now Dasher."

"That was —"

"I'm not through yet. Don't forget Rudolph. And then there's Olive."

"There's no reindeer named Olive, Mr. Masters."

"Sure there is," he said. "Just sing the song. He's Olive the other reindeer, the one who used to laugh and call Rudolph names."

Raker was about to smile when he remembered how tiring it had been to deal with eccentric clients who came to him only because of his success in the Edmonds case.

"How did you find me, Mr. Masters? When you called, you said you knew someone involved in the case against Henry Edmonds."

"Please call me Twirly. All my friends do, and I want you to be my friend. After all, we have so much in common, and —"

Raker cut him off. "I don't mean to be rude, but I have a busy schedule. The question is part of my due diligence in deciding whether to represent you."

"Due diligence. I like that phrase. In layman's terms, doesn't it mean to check things out, be careful, turn over every stone, look before you leap and that type of thing? Am I right? Sure I am. You can't be too careful, can you?"

"No, you can't." Raker thought he hadn't been careful enough when he agreed to meet with Twirly Masters. "So who do you know from the trial? Is it Judy Robertson?" Judy had been the prosecution's main witness, from the county tax department. She had become a good friend to Raker after the trial, even more so after Elizabeth's death.

"No, it wasn't Ms. Robertson. And it wasn't the prosecutor Jason Peabody, the one she married, either."

"Do you know someone in law enforcement? Was it the police officer?"

Masters laughed. "No, it wasn't the police officer."

"Well, if it wasn't Robertson, Peabody or the police officer, who was it?" Then Raker had an idea. "Was it the woman who witnessed the scene at the Tipsy Tavern?"

"No, it wasn't Shelly Barker."

"Then how do you know her name?"

"I know a lot about that trial."

Raker thought about Augustus Langhorne Stark, the judge at the trial, and he shivered. He doubted Judge Stark knew Twirly Masters, but on the other hand, maybe he did and this was a sick joke being played on him by the retired judge.

The other key witnesses at the trial were Hank Snow and Henry Edmonds himself. Snow had wanted to send Henry to jail and ruin Christmas for thousands of children. If Masters was connected in any way to Hank Snow, Raker wanted nothing to do with him.

As if reading his mind, Masters said, "It wasn't Hank Snow."

"But you do know him?" Raker was suddenly suspicious of Masters.

"As I said, I know a lot about that trial. I was there for most of it. On the last day, the courtroom was filled to capacity. What a wonderful day. Don't you think it was a wonderful day? Yes, just spectacular. Anyway, I was there. I had a personal and professional interest in the outcome."

"Meaning what?"

"Meaning that is why I am here." Twirly Masters leaned toward him. "You're thinking about the Patten case, aren't you?"

"Mr. Masters," Raker said, losing patience. "The Patten case was not a good experience for me. I let my heart rule where my head should have urged caution. The newspaper sold a lot of advertising during that trial, and the headlines weren't kind."

"I remember," Masters said. "One headline said: 'Flying-presents defense crashes the case'."

"And your point is what?" Raker asked.

"The Patten case was an unfortunate loss. I bet one of your attorney friends said you can't win them all. Isn't that what they say to make you feel better? I don't know why they say it, because, after all, it *is* possible to win them all. Anyway, yes, I know all about the Patten case, and you should have won."

"But she was not telling the truth," Raker said.

"Oh, but she was telling the truth. She just wasn't believable. And she talked too much." Twirly Masters stopped and smiled. "Like me, she tends to get her mouth running like a motor. That's the reason I hired her. Liked her style, I did."

"You hired Ms. Patten?"

"Yes, I did. I did indeed. What happened was not her fault. There was a sudden emergency and I know what caused it. If you'd had some real evidence, you might have stopped the man responsible. It's too

17

bad. Yes, too bad. He kept right on going and going and going."

"Who kept right on going?"

"Why, Hank Snow, of course."

Raker was discomforted by the second reference to Hank Snow. He was 1 for 2 in trials where Hank Snow was involved. Before the trial, Snow had visited Ms. Patten and suggested she not disclose what had happened, because no one would believe her and it would cause her to lose her case. When Raker learned that Snow wanted the information to remain secret, he was sure they should share it with the jury. Raker had been wrong.

"The jury didn't believe her story about hundreds of Christmas presents falling from the sky, did they? Or her story about unidentified flying objects?" Masters asked.

"It was a little hard to believe, but the story seemed plausible to me after I represented Henry Edmonds. It did happen on Christmas Eve, after all. I thought they had fallen out of the sleigh."

"You didn't have all the facts, Thad."

"And you do?"

Masters lowered his voice. "Hank Snow set you up. Yes, indeed; he set you up good. I have to give the man credit for being sneaky. He knew the jury wouldn't buy her story. But more than that, he knew that if you lost the case, nobody would believe in flying presents and he could continue his work."

Raker waited for Masters to say more.

"But let's not dwell on the past. What's done is done," Masters said. "We need to focus on my case, because we can't let Snow win again, can we?"

"You think Hank Snow is conspiring against you?"

"It's only a hunch. More like a feeling. I need more time to be sure."

Raker studied Masters more closely. "Why are you here?"

"It's like this, Thad. You and I are on the same team. We are both True Believers."

Raker was caught off guard. He became a True Believer during the Edmonds trial and married Elizabeth, but 11 months later, she was gone, along with most of his beliefs. The Patten case killed off the rest.

"I'm not a True Believer," Raker said at last. "Not anymore. So maybe I'm not the lawyer for you."

Masters got out of his chair and walked to the window. Raker could see him looking at the courthouse. He then turned to face Raker.

"Thad, may I offer you some advice? There are two kinds of people, those who believe and those who don't. Some say there is no difference between the lives of believers and nonbelievers, but I have seen the difference with my own eyes, felt it in my heart. Yes, I have. Yes, indeed. Times are not always easy. Tough things happen to good people. Life can hit you hard. You can suffer for reasons that are unexplainable. And there are things you can't control. But I can tell you something that's absolutely, positively wonderful and true. You and only you control your beliefs, and no one can rob you of them. Belief is free. Yes, it is. And maybe, just maybe, if you believe hard enough, you will have a return on investment that cannot be measured or predicted."

Raker was already weary and his day was just getting started. He wanted to tell Twirly Masters to leave but he couldn't do it. He had a feeling, nothing more, but it was one he hadn't experienced since the day he met Henry Edmonds. Raker thought himself the fool, but he decided to hear the man out.

"Tell me your problem, Mr. Masters."

With that, Twirly Masters returned to his seat. He reached inside his coat pocket, pulled out a folded document and handed it to Raker. It was a notice from the county. Raker thumbed through it quickly, long enough to figure out the gist of the matter.

"The county is condemning your property. That's what this is about?"

"I prefer to use the word 'stealing'," Masters said.

"Why does the county want to take your property?"

"They say they want it for a park. Can they do that?"

"They can," Raker said. "With eminent domain, the government can take private property for a public purpose."

For the first time, Masters' affable demeanor was shaken. "You're telling me they can take my property and turn it into a park even though the way I'm using it has more value to the public? That's silly, wrong and shortsighted. It doesn't go down well, I have to tell you. It's kind of like eating cereal with sour milk."

Raker began to think like a lawyer; this was going to be a simple, straightforward case. "Don't worry. They must compensate you and we can hire an expert to get you the highest price possible."

"I don't want the county's money." Masters' voice rose. "There is something much more important here than money. Can't you see that?"

Raker could not see that because the law was clear. Besides, his clients always reacted this way. They were shocked that the government could take their property, and then dismayed at the value the government placed on it. What matters, he would explain to them, is the fair market value of the property, not how much it means to the owner who doesn't want to part with it, because it is always about the money.

"Mr. Masters, I know you say you don't want the money —"

"I don't. No way. No how. I don't even have a bank to put it in. Money won't replace the service I provide at the property."

"I know it may be unsettling to lose your property like this. Has it been in the family a long time?"

"You might say that," Masters said. "About 300 years."

"That is a long time. Can you tell me about the property?"

"It's 90 acres off old Highway 11, across from the Ledbetter farm. There's an old house up on the ridge about half a mile from the road."

"Are you talking about the Haints?" Raker was surprised.

Masters laughed. "That's the name the school kids gave it years ago, and the name stuck. The house does look haunted, and I do like the name, but I can assure you we harbor no ghosts. I have more important things to do."

"When I was a kid," Raker said, "we used to ride our bikes out there, head up the dirt road to the house and peek in the windows. It always looked deserted to me. I can't remember seeing anyone in the house or on the property."

"Good description. It does have that feel to it. But don't you think it's important to keep a low profile when trying to keep secrets?" Masters asked.

"I don't follow," Raker said.

"You weren't supposed to see anyone. Otherwise, it wouldn't be a surprise."

"What wouldn't be a surprise?"

Masters didn't answer the question. "Is there a way I can keep the property? It's very important. Yes, indeed."

Raker turned in his chair and glanced at the statute books on his shelf. He grabbed one and flipped through it until he found the page he wanted. After reading for a few minutes, he set the book down and turned back to face Masters. "There is a process for challenging the condemnation of your property," Raker said, "but the law favors the county."

"All I want is a chance. Will you represent me?"

Raker took a moment to make up his mind. Twirly Masters would be an interesting client. And he liked his passion. "I will," Raker said, "as long as you understand that I am not a miracle worker."

Twirly Masters jumped to his feet and put out his hand. "Ah, but you are a miracle worker, Thad Raker. You saved Christmas once before."

"Now wait a minute," Raker said, while shaking Masters' hand. "This case is not about saving Christmas."

Masters smiled. "Are you sure?" And with that, he reached into his shirt pocket, took out his card and placed it in Raker's hand. "I have to head north for a few days to take care of some business. Call me if you need me."

As Masters left his office, Raker looked at the card. The insignia was a wrapped Christmas present sitting on a sleigh. Masters' contact information was displayed on a Christmas tree. Flipping the card over, Raker saw fine, cursive handwriting that read, "I believe in you."

Same Day in November

2:30 p.m.

Liz Raker was glad to hear the bell ring at the end of the school day. She picked up her book bag and headed for her locker located near a group of chattering girls in her grade. As Liz approached, they glanced at her, and then moved away. Typical, she thought. She grabbed her coat from the locker and headed for the door. Anywhere but here would be fine with her.

It was her birthday and she should have been happy, but she wasn't. Being 11 years old was nothing more than an odd number in an even universe. She didn't fit in at school because she was introspective like her dad and a bookworm like her mother. When she told her dad that she didn't want a birthday party this year, it was because there was no one she wanted to invite. She thought he was relieved. She knew it was hard for him, raising her without her mom.

She pulled her bike from the bike rack and climbed on, careful to avoid patches of melting snowfall. The afternoon temperature was a brisk 35 degrees, but she was well-bundled and the sun was out, so she was happy to take a ride; it gave her a sense of freedom. She pedaled out of the neighborhood and down the sidewalk of a busy street, until she found herself passing near the local mall. Christmas decorations had been up since shortly after Halloween, and they were a reminder; she had been keeping a secret from her dad. Pretty soon, she'd have to tell him that she had serious doubts about the existence of Santa Claus.

Liz had willed herself to continue to believe in Santa Claus for the sake of her father, but she had been struggling with the question for the last six months. It started on the playground in May when a fifth-grader announced to everyone that Santa

Claus was not real. She didn't want to believe it, even pressed her hands against her ears to stop the flow of information, but the arguments just kept coming. Day after day the fifth-grader held court on the playground like a televangelist trying to save the souls of every child in the school. He made good points, which bothered Liz still more. She tried to ask her dad a few questions, such as, how does Santa get to all the homes in the world in one night? He said exactly what the fifth-grader said he would say: It was "magic." But Liz knew about magic. She had received a magic set one year for Christmas, and it was all tricks and gimmicks.

"So is it just a trick?" she asked her dad.

"Not at all," he said, but he had no proof. Liz had to have proof. Besides, her dad was famous as the man who saved Christmas. How could she talk to him?

Her dad had always encouraged her to be her own person, to get the facts and make up her own mind. Over the past few months, Liz had done just that, even doing research on the Internet. But nothing led her to any evidence that Santa Claus was real or that reindeer could fly. When she woke up on her 11th birthday, her mind was 95 percent made up that none of it was real.

As she pedaled and thought about Santa Claus, she heard the squeal of tires and looked ahead just in time to see a small boy dive off his bike to avoid being hit by a car. The driver yelled at him and drove on. Liz rode up to help.

"Are you OK?" she asked. Then she realized the rider was a girl, not a boy.

She was dressed in sneakers, worn blue jeans and a hooded sweatshirt. Her short brown hair was pressed tight to her head. At first, Liz thought she was 5 or 6 because she was so little, but up close, she seemed older, maybe 9.

"Do you see my hat?" the girl asked. Liz looked around. She spotted a baseball cap in the bushes.

"Is this it?" The girl grabbed it, put it on and turned the bill slightly to the right, grinning at Liz as she did.

"What's your name?" Liz asked.

"Holly."

"I'm Elizabeth, but I go by Liz. Do you need any help?"

"I'm good," Holly said.

"But your knee is bleeding," Liz said. She took a bandana out of her pocket and, together, they rolled up the leg of Holly's jeans and wrapped it around the cut. "Do you live near here?"

"Not too far," she said.

"Can I ride along with you to make sure nothing is wrong with your bike?"

"Fine with me," Holly said, "if you can keep up." She bounced up and down, shook herself off and straddled her bike, balancing on her tiptoes. When she took off, Liz followed, pedaling hard to keep up. Liz thought she was going to like Holly.

Twenty minutes later, they had ridden out of the busy part of town, into the country. They took a curve and slowed down, turning off the highway onto a dirt road that disappeared into a row of trees. They both stopped at the entrance.

"Where are we? Liz asked.

"Home," Holly said.

"But I don't see a house."

"There." Holly pointed through a small opening in the trees toward the top of a hill.

Sure enough, through a gap in the trees, Liz could see a rolling meadow that went up to the top of a hill. On the ridge was on old house.

"I think I've heard of this place," Liz said. "Isn't this the Haints?"

Holly laughed. "That's what Twirly likes people to call it, 'cause it makes people scared and keeps them away." She started riding up the dirt road.

Liz paused. She was supposed to be at her Aunt Laura's for her birthday dinner, but she couldn't give up a chance to take a quick peek at the Haints.

"Wait up." She pedaled hard to catch up.

Holly waited for her near a house that looked cold and empty. The Haints was two stories, with three chimneys, and three dormer windows sticking out of a steep-pitched roof. The outside walls of the first story were made out of large stones and the walls of the second story were made of fading planks. There were a lot of windows on both stories, but their shutters were broken and they were missing panes of glass. It gave Liz the creeps.

"Are your parents at work?" she asked.

"I don't have any. I have Twirly. He looks after me and everyone else."

"So, there are other people here?" Liz asked.

"Yep. There's a whole bunch of us."

"I don't understand."

Holly answered with a question. "Do you believe in Santa Claus?"

Liz was puzzled. "I used to, but I'm not sure now."

"Well, I believe in Santa Claus."

Liz remembered when she believed 100 percent in Santa Claus, so she decided to be encouraging. "I'm glad you believe in Santa Claus."

Holly grinned. "I should. I work for him."

"What did you say?"

The baseball cap on Holly's head had worked its way around to sit the way it was meant, so she adjusted the bill to the right again. She looked Liz in the eye.

"Let's go in."

"I can't," Liz said. Holly stopped and looked back. "I have to be somewhere for dinner. Can we do it another time?"

"Any time," Holly said. She reached into her pocket, took out a small card and handed it to Liz.

"What's this?" Liz asked.

"My union training card. Isn't it cool?"

Liz had never heard of a kid having a business card, so she took a close look at it. On the top left of the card, it said, "North Pole Enterprises — Zone 24 Station." To the right was an insignia of a wrapped Christmas present sitting on a sleigh. At the bottom of the card, it said "Holly Elftobe" and there was an email address below the name that read, "Hollyelftobe@elfmail.com."

"Just email me at that address when you want to visit. I'm always here, unless I'm running an errand for Twirly."

"I don't understand," Liz said. "You're too young to have a job."

"I'm older than I look. Plus, my left ear is getting more pointed every day. I turn my hat to the right, so it shows. See?" She pulled at her left ear as she leaned toward Liz.

Liz didn't see anything unusual. But the name on the card was one she'd never heard. "Is Elftobe a family name?"

"All trainees in the company have that last name. Elf-To-Be."

It was getting dark when Liz arrived at her Aunt Laura's house. When she rode up the driveway, her dad pulled in behind her. She jumped off her bike and ran to meet him.

"Hey, birthday girl. How was your day?"

"Kind of strange. I met an elf-in-training who says she works for Santa Claus."

After dinner, Liz and her dad rode home together, her bike in the trunk of his car. She brought up the subject she had been dreading. "Daddy, I'm having a hard time believing in Santa Claus this year."

"What's the problem?"

"Lots of things. Elves. Magic. Flying reindeer. Getting to all the houses in one night. I just don't see how it's possible."

She saw him smile. "What about the elf-in-training you met today? Don't you have some proof now?"

"She's just a little girl, Daddy. She's supposed to have an imagination."

He was quiet for a moment. "I understand what you're going through. When I was your age, I stopped believing, too."

"What happened to change your mind later?"

"I met your mother and then I met Henry Edmonds. But since we're being honest with each other, I need to admit something, too. I'm not the believer I was when I married your mother."

"I feel bad, Daddy," Liz said. "I still love the story. I'm sorry."

"There is nothing to be sorry about. You need to make up your own mind about what you believe. How you were named should have nothing to do with it. And as for the story about that trial, well, it's just that, a story. Sometimes the truth will hit you in the face, and you just have to learn to live with it."

December 7ᵗʰ

9:30 am

Raker met Twirly Masters at the entrance to the courthouse. They went through security and caught the elevator to the fourth floor.

"What a beautiful day, just fabulous. I was telling everyone at the Haints this morning how nice it is, and to be sure to get outside. They need to breathe it, the air I mean. It's just so fresh, don't you think, Thad?"

Raker had ridden the courthouse elevator more than a thousand times over the years and nothing about it felt beautiful, fabulous or fresh. The day?

Maybe. But the impending court hearing gave him an uneasy feeling and the quality of the air outside of the building wouldn't be of any help. Most lawyers, even the good ones, are nervous before a hearing. But that wasn't the reason Raker felt the way he did; the motion he would be arguing was as thin as a communion wafer.

"Please tell me again the name of the motion you filed," Masters said.

"It's called a motion for injunctive relief," Raker explained.

"Yes. Yes. I like the sound of that," Masters said. "Sounds Latin, but I suppose most legal words have a Latin origin. Sounds kind of harsh, too. Good. That's good. Let me guess. Don't tell me. You are moving to make them stop."

"Yes," Raker said. "This is a motion to enjoin, or, as you put it, stop the county from taking your property."

"Splendid. I knew you were the man for the job," Masters replied. "You just tell the judge what's what and I keep my property, right?"

"It's not that simple. The county will have a lawyer who will argue that taking the property for a park is about as basic a public purpose as it gets."

"Not a problem, Thad Raker. I have faith in you."

The elevator stopped on the fourth floor and Raker was glad to see they had 20 minutes to spare. He made it a habit to be early to court, so he had a chance to calm himself. With Twirly Masters as a client, he'd need every second.

A few minutes later, they were seated together in Courtroom 4112. Except for them, the room was empty. The next person to arrive was the clerk. Raker walked up to say hello.

"Shirley, do you know who will be the judge today?"

"Oh, I think I'll let that be a surprise, Mr. Raker."

He knew Shirley had a sense of humor, but surprises were uncommon for her.

At exactly 10:00 a.m., a young bailiff entered the courtroom. "The judge wants to know if all the parties are ready."

Raker stood up. "Mr. Masters is ready. I haven't seen the county's attorney yet."

The bailiff went back through the same door and, as it shut, Raker heard a loud voice from the other side expressing displeasure. Shirley hid her face behind her computer screen but Raker saw her smile.

At 10:15, the main courtroom door banged open and Raker turned to see a parade of lawyers carrying briefcases, easels, laptops and posters. In the lead, carrying nothing but his broad chest puffed out three times more than necessary, was Cleve R. Johnson, Esquire, head of the most prestigious law firm in the county. Raker knew him by sight and by reputation but had never been opposite him in court. Johnson got to him before Raker could stand to shake hands, put his hand on Raker's shoulder to keep him seated and leaned over him like a buzzard admiring fresh kill.

"Cleve R. Johnson, representing the county. Glad to meet you, Thad. Heard a lot about you. Santa Claus and all."

Johnson left his perch above Raker and began directing traffic, pointing here and there and shouting instructions. He tossed his overcoat to one of his lackeys, motioned for someone to hand him a small briefcase and then took his seat, ready to proceed and looking rather impatient.

Twirly Masters turned in his chair to face Raker. "One against six, Thad. I like our chances."

It wasn't the odds that bothered Raker. It was the lawyer who was seated second chair for the county, Sarah Kennedy. It didn't feel right to oppose her, and he knew she was a darned good lawyer.

"She's very attractive, Thad," Masters said. "Yes, tiptop."

Before Raker could respond, the bailiff re-entered the courtroom and stood at attention, a signal for everyone to stop talking. Raker imagined himself in the eye of a hurricane, with the worst part of the storm yet to arrive. He couldn't have been more right.

Just then the side door blew open and in walked the judge. Raker swallowed hard. Was this really happening? When this judge retired — after the "trial of the century," 12 years earlier — Raker and most of the lawyers in the county had expelled a collective sigh of relief. It seemed Lady Justice had a sense of humor.

"Oyez, oyez, oyez, this honorable court of this great state is now open for business. Judge Augustus Langhorne Stark, presiding. Be seated and come to order." The bailiff folded his cheat sheet and sat down in a chair against the wall, ready to watch the show.

Everyone followed suit except for Cleve. R. Johnson, Esquire.

"Good morning, your honor," Johnson said. "It is a pleasure to see you again. You must be filling in for Judge Davidson. I'd heard he had an accident. We are grateful to have you on the bench in this case." Johnson sat down, clearly pleased with these opening remarks.

Judge Stark ignored him and turned his attention to Raker. "Good morning, Mr. Raker."

"Morning, your honor."

"It's been a while, hasn't it?"

"Yes, sir." He was cautious. Twelve years earlier, Judge Stark hadn't been nearly this friendly.

"Mr. Johnson." Judge Stark turned full focus on the man.

"Yes, your honor."

"Do you have a watch?"

"Excuse me?"

"Simple question: Do you have a watch?"

"Why, yes, sir, I do." Johnson raised his left arm and revealed a Rolex with diamond clusters.

"Does it work?"

"Why yes, sir, it does."

"I'm not sure that it does," Judge Stark said. "I'd like to inspect it. Bailiff."

The bailiff got up and walked toward Johnson, his hand out to receive the timepiece.

Johnson delivered the watch and tugged his coat sleeve down over his wrist. "Whatever you like, your honor, but I just don't understand the reason. The watch works fine."

The bailiff handed the watch to Judge Stark. "Thank you for that admission, Mr. Johnson. One other question: Did you have this with you all morning?" Judge Stark was holding the watch up for Johnson to see.

"I did, your honor."

"Very good," Judge Stark said. "Madam court reporter, did you get all that?" The court reporter responded that she did and Raker saw that the slick veneer that was Cleve R. Johnson, Esquire, had lost some of its luster.

"Mr. Johnson, I am placing you in conditional contempt of court and remanding your watch as evidence if needed later in a contempt proceeding."

Johnson shot up. "What? You can't —"

"Hold on, Mr. Johnson." Judge Stark held up his right hand, the palm facing Johnson. "The word 'conditional' is in this ruling for a reason. You have been warned."

Raker wondered if any judge had ever spoken to Cleve R. Johnson in this fashion. He was past president of both the local and state bar associations, and everyone in the legal community showed him deference. Judges running for office often asked for his endorsement, and he was well-respected on the national stage. Judges usually took his word as gospel. But now Johnson stood facing a cantankerous judge who could not care less about his reputation. The encounter lifted Raker's spirits. It certainly did.

"Mr. Johnson, you and I aren't too far apart in age," Judge Stark said. "I have about 10 years on you, and though you may not remember, when I was on the bench in my mid-30s, I gave a speech to the young lawyers' association and you were there. In fact, you were their president. I handed out copies of what I called 'Judge Stark's Rules of Court.' Did you lose your copy?"

"I'm sorry, your honor, I don't remember. I am sure it was an excellent —"

"Rule 1. That's the rule you forgot," Judge Stark said. "I can understand forgetting Rule 6 or Rule 9, but Rule 1? Really, Mr. Johnson, I expected more from a man of your intellect."

"Judge Stark, is there something I have done to offend you?"

"Bingo, Mr. Johnson. You violated Rule 1. You made the judge in this case, me, wait 15 minutes on you. I don't wait on you. You don't run this courtroom. Do you understand these very basic concepts?"

Cleve R. Johnson was red in the face. He paused to gather himself. "Your honor, do you think perhaps we got off on the wrong foot?"

"Is that an apology?"

Johnson had not intended to make an apology, but he was stuck. "Your honor, I apologize for being late and want you to know that unless I am dead or in the hospital, it won't happen again."

"Sounds good to me. Now, if the parties are ready to proceed, we need introductions for the record."

Raker stood. "Thad Raker, attorney for T. W. Masters."

"Cleve R. Johnson, with the law firm of Johnson, Brakeman & Walker, attorneys for the county."

Raker detected a hint of emphasis on the lead name of the law firm and saw that Johnson's chest was beginning to inflate again. He had a hunch Judge Stark would not be impressed.

"Mr. Johnson, it looks like you have Mr. Raker outnumbered. Would you care to introduce all your helpers for the record?"

"Absolutely, your honor. I have with me today my junior partner, Sarah Kennedy, and my associates Ken Madden and Bill McCullough. Also with me is my paralegal, Rick McDonald. And then we have. . ." Johnson looked at Sarah Kennedy who had scribbled a note for him. "Ah, yes. Wyatt Stokes. Mr. Stokes is. . ."

"Helping you carry your stuff," Judge Stark offered.

"Yes, sir, that's our team, and we are here to represent the county in what is a simple and straightforward hearing."

"Really," Judge Stark said. "I would hate to see how many lawyers you need to handle a complex hearing."

Raker looked across at the county's team of lawyers and bowed his head slightly to Kennedy. She nodded a salute in return. With her on the county's team, he knew he was in for a challenge. It felt like David versus Goliath, but even David had a sling. All Raker had was Twirly Masters, the man who had mastered the reindeer test, backward.

Masters passed a note to Raker. "Breathe, Thad."

"As Mr. Johnson suggested," Judge Stark said to the room at large, "I am serving in an emergency status. Judge Davidson fell from the top of a tall ladder until the ground broke his fall and most of the bones in his left leg; he will be out for a month. The chief judge dug deep and I was her fifth choice. I had to decide between spending time in this wonderful courtroom and watching the Weather Channel. It was a close call, but I figured the next month will be cold and wet, so I wouldn't miss much. Who would like to tell me why we are here today?"

Cleve R. Johnson was on his feet before Raker could move. "Your honor, I don't mean to speak ill of my colleague, but he has filed a frivolous motion. Pursuant to applicable law and in accordance with the unanimous vote of the county commission, the county is exercising its constitutional power of eminent domain to condemn Mr. Masters' property to build a park. As this court well knows, and Mr. Raker should, too, the statute plainly states that taking land for a park is a valid public purpose. We don't think this hearing should last long."

"Where is the property?"

"It's on Highway 11, in the southern part of the county," Johnson said. "Consists of 90 acres, more or less."

"Are you talking about the Haints?" Judge Stark asked.

Johnson looked around to his team. Kennedy whispered in his ear. "I believe, yes, your honor, some people call it by that name."

"Why in the world would the county want to put a park out there?" Judge Stark asked. "Are you looking to entertain cows?"

Raker heard his cue. "We have the same question, your honor. Highway 11 is out of the way. There are numerous places better than the Haints

44

to place a park in this county, if that truly is the intention."

"Truly the intention?" Judge Stark asked. "Are you suggesting the county doesn't intend to use the property for a park?"

"If it please the court," Raker said, "we would like to call several witnesses to address the legality of the taking."

"We object," Johnson said. "Mr. Raker is well-known for his courtroom theatrics, but calling witnesses on a legal point so clear is a waste of the taxpayer's money."

"I expect at your hourly billing rate, Mr. Johnson, that is probably true," Judge Stark said. "Nonetheless, I would rather hear witnesses testify about the Haints than watch reruns of 'The Beverly Hillbillies,' so let's get on with it. Call your first witness, Mr. Raker."

Masters slapped Raker on the back, as if victory must be close at hand. What Raker knew that Twirly didn't was that Judge Stark could turn on either side at any time. But for now, Raker had won a skirmish and had to make the most of it.

"We call Clyde Driscole, the county manager," Raker said.

Raker had subpoenaed Driscole, who was sitting in the pew behind Johnson's team. When he stood to make his way to the witness stand, Johnson said, "For the record, your honor, we object strenuously to this ploy. Mr. Driscole's time is important. The state Supreme Court has said it's legal to take property for a park. Why we are here is a mystery."

"Mr. Johnson," Judge Stark held up Johnson's expensive watch. "If you want to make an objection for the record, once is enough. If you keep popping up and down like the mole in Whack-A-Mole every time things don't go your way, you are going to violate Judge Stark's Rule 7, and that won't make me very happy. Do we understand each other?"

Raker listened to this exchange and thought the judge's mood hadn't improved in retirement.

As Clyde Driscole was being sworn in, Raker took a deep breath. He didn't know how this gamble would work out, but he looked over his notes and renewed his vow to do the best he could for his client.

"Mr. Driscole, good morning."

"Good morning, sir."

"You have been the county manager for 25 years, correct?"

"Twenty-six, but who's counting?"

"Very good," Raker said. "Long enough to see a few condemnation cases."

"Quite a few." Driscole was a man of few words. Either that or he had been well-coached by the legion of lawyers on the other side of the courtroom.

"Am I correct," Raker asked, "that most of the takings of private property by the county during your tenure have been for transportation-related projects, such as roads and sidewalks?"

"True," Driscole said.

"And is it also true that the only takings during your tenure having anything to do with outdoor activities for public enjoyment have been partial takings for the greenway bike and walking paths in the center of town?"

"Yes."

"So why 90 acres off Highway 11, far from town? And why now?"

"We thought it was time to provide the community with a nice park," Driscole said.

"What kind of park?"

"That is still in the planning stages," Driscole replied.

"In fact," Raker said, "the park you are proposing to put on my client's land is not part of the county's master plan, is it?"

"We are continually modifying that plan." Driscole seemed a bit defensive for the first time.

"Aren't those modifications required to be posted on the county's website?"

Driscole looked to his lawyers, and then back at Raker. "I suppose so."

"I supposed so, too," Raker said, "which is why I looked for the modification to the plan. Is there some reason I couldn't find it on your website?"

"Like I said, we are still in the planning stages."

"But I thought the county had an orderly process for such things," Raker offered. "As I recall, there were a number of public meetings related to the greenway, several debates before the county commission, and the maps for the project were posted, modified and then reposted before any private land was taken."

Johnson jumped in. "Objection, your honor. That's not a question. Mr. Raker is simply giving a speech."

"Do you have a question for Mr. Driscole, Mr. Raker?" Judge Stark asked.

"Yes, your honor." Turning back to the witness, Raker asked: "Mr. Driscole, can you explain why there were no public meetings for a 90-acre park, no maps posted for public review and no debate by the county commission?"

"We weren't obligated to have public meetings and there was nothing to debate. It's the perfect site for a park. And it's fair to Mr. Masters." Driscole looked to Johnson, who nodded his approval.

"Perfect and fair, you say?" Raker asked.

"Yes, the tax records show the structures are worth $10,000 and the land is worth $1,000 per acre. For $100,000, payable to your client, the county will get the land to build a nice park for the residents of this community."

"Move to strike, your honor," Raker said. "The tax value is not admissible to prove fair market value of the property."

Raker glanced across the aisle and saw Sarah Kennedy whispering to Johnson, who then rose. "Your honor, the testimony is proper because it demonstrates why the county voted to condemn Mr. Masters' property; it is not offered to demonstrate the fair market value of the property. Once the court denies Mr. Raker's motion to enjoin, we will be glad to have an expert testify about the value of the property."

Judge Stark sustained the objection and Raker was reminded again of Sarah Kennedy's legal skills. He pressed forward.

"Mr. Driscole, you didn't have anyone from the county inspect the property before the county commissioners voted, did you?"

"No."

"And you didn't get an appraisal on the property first, did you?"

"As I said, I knew the tax value." Driscole made it sound like he was teaching a student.

"But isn't it typical, before voting to condemn, for the county to inspect the property and hire an appraiser to value the property?"

"That is typical," Driscole acknowledged. "But I didn't feel it was necessary."

"So you made that decision?" Raker asked.

"Yes."

Raker moved to another topic. "Did you prepare the agenda for the county commission meeting?"

"I did," Driscole said.

"And when did you provide it to the commissioners?" Raker asked.

"We do that two days before the meeting."

"But the motion to take my client's property was not on the agenda you provided to the commissioners two days before the September meeting, was it?"

Driscole looked to Johnson, who helped with an upright objection. "Your honor, this line of questioning is entirely irrelevant. We object."

Judge Stark thought for a moment and said, "Mr. Johnson, because you were 15 minutes late, I am going to give Mr. Raker a little more time to demonstrate the relevance." He held up Cleve R. Johnson's Rolex, turned to Raker and said, "Mr. Raker, the watch is ticking."

"Mr. Driscole, please answer the question."

"I don't recall," Driscole said.

After getting Judge Stark's permission, Raker approached Driscole and placed a document in front of him. "Do you recognize this document, Mr. Driscole?"

Driscole took a moment to read it, then said, "Yes, this is the agenda for the September meeting."

"Do you see anything on it about the taking of my client's property?"

"No," Driscole responded.

"Does that refresh your recollection about what happened?"

"I have a large staff assisting me."

"I see," Raker said. "Well, let me show you another document. Do you recognize it?"

Driscole held the sheet of paper in his hand as he studied it. Raker continued, "Let me help you, Mr. Driscole. This is an amended agenda for the September meeting with your signature, isn't it?"

"It is," Driscole replied.

"And the date on this document is the same day as the September county commission meeting, correct?"

"Correct," Driscole said.

"And this document reflects the addition of one item to the agenda that night, a motion to take my client's property, doesn't it?"

"It does," Driscole said.

"When during the day of the meeting did you decide to add this item to the agenda?"

"I don't recall." Driscole shifted in his chair.

"Just to recap," Raker said. "The vote to take my client's property was not planned until the day of the September meeting, and before the vote occurred, no public meetings had been held about the park, no amendments had been made to the master plan, no maps had been prepared for the park and no inspections or appraisals had been done of the property to be used for the park. Did I get that right?"

Driscole looked to Johnson again, but before Johnson could leap to his defense, Judge Stark said, "Mr. Driscole, Mr. Johnson is not going to answer the question for you."

Driscole looked at the two documents again, and said, "What you say about the process is accurate. We saw an opportunity to enrich the lives of the residents of this county, and we took it."

"In secret?" Raker asked.

"What do you mean?"

"By discussing the motion in closed session that night," Raker said.

Cleve R. Johnson was on his feet. "Objection, your honor. Legal matters discussed in closed session are not subject to disclosure."

Judge Stark thought a moment and then said, "Sustained, for the time being. If it becomes apparent that the discussion was about more than legal matters affecting the park, we can revisit this issue. Move on, Mr. Raker."

"Your honor," Raker said, "how will I be able to determine whether additional information was discussed in closed session if I can't ask what was discussed?"

"Not my problem, Mr. Raker. Bring me some law or bring me some facts. Otherwise, move on."

Raker gathered his composure. "Mr. Driscole, was there a lawyer who went into closed session with you?"

"Objection," Johnson said.

"Overruled. The names of the persons present at the closed session are not protected from disclosure."

"You may answer, Mr. Driscole," Raker said. "Was there a lawyer at the closed session?"

"Yes, sir."

"Who was it?"

"Mr. Johnson."

"The same Mr. Johnson who is representing the county in this proceeding?"

"Yes, sir."

"And," Raker continued, "was the sole topic of the closed session that night the taking of my client's property?"

Driscole paused until Judge Stark Stark began to stir. "Yes," Driscole said.

"Just a few more questions, Mr. Driscole. When the commissioners came out of closed session and took a vote on the motion to condemn my client's property, was there any discussion of that motion before the public?"

"I don't believe so," Driscole said. "All the commissioners were for it. Further discussion would have been a waste of time."

"Because it had all been sorted out in closed session?"

"Objection." Johnson was furious. "Your honor, he is trying to violate your ruling. You should hold *him* in conditional contempt of court."

"Mr. Johnson," Judge Stark said. "You must stop telling me what I should do. Now sit down and be quiet. Mr. Raker, do you have any final questions?"

Raker put his hand on Twirly Masters' shoulder and looked at the witness. "Mr. Driscole, why didn't you notify my client of the September meeting? Were you worried that if you did, the commissioners might not help you ram this thing through?"

"Objection," Johnson said. "The law does not require notice to the landowner before the vote to condemn the property is taken."

"Is that true, Mr. Raker?" Judge Stark asked.

"Your honor, it is customary for the county to contact the property owner to try to resolve the matter before voting to condemn the property. Legally, I admit, it is not required."

"The objection is sustained," Judge Stark said. "Do you have anything further for this witness, Mr. Raker?"

"Not at this time, your honor."

"What about you, Mr. Johnson?" Judge Stark asked.

"No, your honor."

"We'll take a 15-minute break," Judge Stark said.

The judge left the room quickly and Masters leaned over to Raker and said, "Well done, Thad. Mighty sneaky stuff going on there and you brought it out. Yes, you did."

Raker didn't feel worthy of the praise. "Excuse me, Twirly. I need to make a phone call." He headed to the hallway to make his call but was intercepted in the aisle by Johnson.

"Your client should settle this case," Johnson said. "If he keeps fighting, he won't get much for the property. But because he seems like a nice guy, I will recommend that the county pay a little more than tax value. He should take it."

Raker looked back at Twirly, and then to Johnson. "I don't think he is very interested in your advice, Mr. Johnson. But I'll let him know you think he's nice. That should lift his spirits. Now, if you will excuse me, I have a call to make."

December 7th

11:15 a.m.

During the break, Raker called his friend Judy Robertson, who was now property tax manager for the county. He had told her about his new case and she had offered to look up the public tax records on Masters' property.

"How's it going?" Judy asked.

"It could be better," Raker said. "For starters, the judge is Augustus Stark."

"I thought he retired."

"So did everybody else," Raker said. "So, what have you got for me?"

"Your client has been listed as the taxpayer of record for the last 45 years and he has never been late on his taxes. But there is one thing that is curious," Robertson said.

"What is that?"

"He isn't the owner of the property. It's owned by a company called NPE, LLC. When I saw that, I checked the public record in the Register of Deeds and found a memorandum of lease on file showing that NPE, LLC leased the property to your client."

"What kind of lease?" Raker asked.

"It's a long-term lease, 45 years."

Raker wondered why Masters hadn't given him that information. "At least he has leasehold rights to the property," Raker said. "If he didn't, there wouldn't be much to fight about."

"There's something else," Judy said. "This will affect your case. The lease expires this month, on December 21st."

So Twirly Masters wasn't just an odd client. He was an odd client who withheld important information from his attorney.

Raker didn't know what to make of the news, so he asked about the tax value. "Do you think the value is low?"

"Don't think so," Judy said. "When we did the last countywide property tax valuation, we looked closely at the rural properties. I think the tax value on the property is pretty close to what an appraiser will say it's worth, even a hired gun."

So Clyde Driscole had been correct about the property's fair market value. "Anything else?" he asked.

"Well, there is one thing."

"Something else in the public record?"

"No. It was someone I saw."

"Who?"

"You remember the little man at our trial?" Judy asked.

Raker felt tightness in his chest. "You mean Hank Snow?"

"I saw him yesterday. He went into the county manager's office."

"You saw Hank Snow go into Clyde Driscole's office?"

"Yes. Don't you think that's strange?" Judy asked.

There were no words to describe how Raker felt, but if he had to pick one, strange would work.

"OK, Judy. Thanks for the help."

"Before you go," she said, "I know Sarah's on the legal team representing the county. Tell her I said hi."

"I doubt we will have much time for small talk."

"You should," Judy said. "It's time, Thad."

"Thanks," Raker said, "but my time is full raising a daughter and tilting at windmills." He said goodbye and turned off his phone. He then turned around and walked straight into the side of Sarah Kennedy, knocking the papers she was carrying to the floor. They bent down at the same time to pick them up and found themselves looking at one another, only a few inches separating their faces.

"Hello, Thad," Sarah said.

"Sorry, Sarah. I didn't see you coming. My fault. Let me help."

"Are you OK?"

"I'm fine. Just a lot of things on my mind at the moment."

"Understood," Sarah said. "How is Liz?"

"She's growing up faster than my learning curve can handle."

"Maybe I can help," Sarah said.

"She likes you," Raker said. "That's a nice offer." He didn't know what to say next.

"Well," Sarah said, "I guess we should get back to it."

Raker held the door open for Sarah to enter first.

"Such a gentleman," Sarah said with a smile. "Will you be holding the door for my boss, too?"

"He has enough people to do that for him." He looked around to be sure no one could overhear. "I don't know why you work for him, Sarah."

"Not enough time for that conversation today. Let's go do our jobs and then maybe we can have a drink."

"I don't want you to get fired for hanging out with the enemy."

"But you're not the enemy, Thad. And besides, I can take care of myself."

"I never doubted that," Raker said.

They had 30 seconds to spare, so they hustled to their seats. Cleve R. Johnson was already seated. He was a lot of things, but he didn't appear to be stupid enough to tempt fate with the judge holding onto his expensive watch.

Twirly Masters sat where Raker had left him and, for once, had nothing to say. He appeared to be thinking about something. Maybe he was thinking he should have told his lawyer about the lease.

Judge Stark entered before the young bailiff could do his "all rise" routine. As he took his seat, the bailiff announced, "Be seated and come to order."

"Anything else from your side, Mr. Raker?" Judge Stark asked. "Yes, sir. We have the six county commissioners under subpoena and —"

Johnson came out of his chair as if it had bitten him. "We strenuously object, your honor!"

"Mr. Johnson, do you have an objection that is not strenuous?" Judge Stark snapped.

"Not in this case, your honor. Mr. Raker is making a mockery of the process. Not only is he wasting the court's time complaining about the use of public money for a park, he now wants to drag every single county commissioner into this proceeding to ask why the people might want to have a park. Today, I filed a motion to quash all six subpoenas. I have a copy for the court."

"Did you serve Mr. Raker with the motion?"

"Yes, sir. We hand-delivered it to his office on our way to court this morning."

"That was convenient," Judge Stark said. "While Mr. Raker was here early for the hearing, you were dropping off a copy of your motion at his office. Do you at least have an extra copy you can share with him now?"

Johnson turned to one of his assistants and came up with a copy that he handed to Raker. After a brief review of the motion, Raker stood to address the court.

"Your honor, Mr. Johnson doesn't cite a rule of procedure. He simply argues that it is not appropriate for me to ask any questions of these witnesses."

"That true, Mr. Johnson?" Judge Stark asked.

"Your honor," Johnson said, "the law does not allow Mr. Raker to go on a fishing expedition, which is exactly what he is trying to do."

"What are you fishing for, Mr. Raker?" The judge peered over his glasses.

Raker felt bold. "Just more fish stories like the one we heard from Mr. Driscole. I believe my limit is seven, which is all I plan to catch today."

"Outrageous," Johnson said. "I have never heard such a thing from a young lawyer. How disrespectful. Mr. Raker, someone should teach you a lesson."

With that, Judge Stark's gavel came down hard. "Mr. Johnson, in my courtroom, you address your comments to me, not the other lawyer. If you and Raker want to get into a fistfight after you leave my courtroom, so be it, but right now, I am in charge, not you. Can you get that into that Ivy League head of yours, or do I need to send the bailiff over to put you in handcuffs?"

The bailiff stood up and reached for the cuffs that hung on his belt. The judge held up a hand to stop him and the room got quiet. Judge Stark was thinking.

After a few moments, Judge Stark looked at Johnson and asked, "Where are the six witnesses?"

"At their jobs," Johnson said. "We told them they would be called only if needed."

"So, on your instruction, they did not make themselves available after receiving their subpoenas?"

"We believed you would not require them to testify. The law is so clear on this point, no judge would . . ." Johnson caught himself, but not in time.

"No judge would do what?" Judge Stark asked.

Johnson hesitated, and Judge Stark moved in. "Tell you what this judge is going to do, Mr. Johnson. I am going to listen to the legal arguments of both sides, and then I will make my decision."

"Very well, your honor. Ms. Kennedy will present our argument."

With Johnson seated, Sarah Kennedy rose and laid out the county's case. She discussed several legal precedents that favored the county. In summing up, she said it didn't matter whether the decision to use Mr. Masters' land for a park was good or bad, only that it was to be used for a park, a valid public purpose.

Raker knew she had a good argument and he had only one option, which was the option he planned from the beginning. "The county's process was arbitrary and capricious," he said. "Mr. Driscole admitted that the county normally adheres to certain reasonable and customary steps. Not this time. There was no inspection. No appraisal. No master-plan amendment. No maps. No notice. No attempt to follow an orderly process when taking private property." Raker summed up his argument with reference to a few legal precedents of his own, but he feared they were not as strong as the ones cited by Kennedy.

Judge Stark shuffled some papers on the bench in front of him and then looked up at the attorneys. "Thank you for your presentations. Of the two arguments, Ms. Kennedy, I believe you are correct. A park is a valid public purpose, meaning that the law strongly favors the county's case."

Raker felt deflated but not surprised. He looked at Twirly, who didn't seem affected by the judge's statement. He just sat there quietly, with his usual air of expecting only good things.

"However," Judge Stark said, and that one word renewed Raker's spirit.

"However," the judge repeated, "the facts are important, too, and Mr. Raker was unable to present all the facts because Mr. Johnson didn't bring the county commissioners with him. One option is to have them hauled into court now, but I think I have a better idea." He turned from Johnson to Raker.

"Mr. Raker, if your client loses this motion, does he want a jury trial to determine the amount of money the county must pay him to take his property?"

With the talk of money, Raker noticed that Masters became agitated and was about to speak, so he clamped a hand on his client's shoulder. He had a feeling the judge was about to toss Twirly a lifeline and he didn't want Twirly to say anything that might cause the judge to retract it. "If it comes to that, then yes, your honor. We want a trial."

"Mr. Johnson?" Judge Stark asked. "Are you ready to proceed with a trial?"

"We're ready, your honor."

"So here's what we're going to do," Judge Stark said. "I am setting this case for trial two weeks from today, Monday, December 21st. I will decide if the county has the right to take the property and, if it does, the jury you select will decide how much the land is worth. Mr. Johnson, make sure any commissioners who are subpoenaed know how to find the courtroom. Any questions?"

"Isn't that a little close to Christmas?" Johnson asked.

Judge Stark looked at Raker and smiled. "It's not the first time I've had a trial close to Christmas." With that, he left the courtroom.

Raker exhaled, and realized he hadn't taken a full breath all day. He looked to his client and wondered whether Masters understood what had just happened.

"Do you have any questions?"

"Yes," Masters said. "How did you become such a good lawyer?"

December 7ᵗʰ

Lunchtime

Raker took Masters to lunch because he needed to explain why he shouldn't withhold facts from his lawyer. And then to get the information he needed about the lease.

As they settled into a booth at the Knife and Fork, Twirly Masters smiled his biggest smile. "This has been a very fine day, inside and out. We started with a spirited day in court capped by an invigorating walk to lunch. Yes, indeed. It could be raining, sleeting or snowing, but it's not. Then again, there is beauty in those days, too, don't you think?"

"Twirly, I can't represent you unless you tell me everything," Raker said.

"Now, Thad. If I gave you all the facts at once, your face might explode."

"What?"

"Just an expression I heard the other day," Masters said. "I don't really see how one's face can explode when one's mind fills up with too much information. I suspect one's head could explode but not just his face. Anyway, you have to admit, the expression does paint a picture."

"Did it occur to you that the existence of a lease that is about to expire might be an important fact for me to know?" Raker asked.

"I did," Masters said, "but I didn't think the lease would be a problem. I sense from your expression I was wrong."

"When the lease expires this month, that will be a problem," Raker said.

"But it was extended," Masters said. "Signed, sealed and delivered by Hank Snow himself. It's just that, well, I can't find it."

"Wait a minute. Hank Snow? What does he have to do with your property? And why didn't you tell me the lease was extended and you can't find it?"

"Hank Snow works for the company that leased the property to me," Masters said. "And I didn't tell you, because I didn't want you to worry."

Raker ran back through his conversation with Judy Robertson. And then it hit him. She said the property was leased to Masters by a company named NPE, LLC.

"North Pole Enterprises, LLC," Raker said.

"You are one bright lawyer, Thad Raker. I did well to hire you. And I feel like I am in really good hands with you. Yes, really good hands."

"Hold on," Raker said. "Hank Snow testified 12 years ago that North Pole Enterprises is an international toy company. Why would it own the Haints?"

"That was one whopper of a lie he told, yes, it was, but that's Hank Snow, always worried about the public learning the truth. I don't have to tell you that. You caught him lying when you became a True Believer." Masters hesitated. "Have things changed so much for you since then?" He sounded sad, as if a close friend had delivered bad news.

Raker sighed. Had things changed so much? Well, yes, they had, and being a True Believer was far in his past. "I don't know what to believe anymore."

"Thad, I believe this case will open your eyes again."

"I'm not sure how. You can't find the lease extension. There won't be much of a case without it."

"Then we'll just have to find it, won't we? I will bring in reinforcements to help me. Matter of fact, that's it, I will put my best trainee on it this afternoon. When she sets her mind to something, she's unstoppable. Younger than the others but topnotch. She'll find it."

December 7ᵗʰ

3:15 p.m.

When Liz arrived at the Haints for the second time, the property looked as vacant as it had before. Holly's email said to come to the back door and ring the doorbell, so she leaned her bike against the house, just below a grease-stained window. Peering through it, she saw no lights, just dark shadows cast by the afternoon sun. The back entry had a screen door hanging on loose hinges. She wondered if it was safe to enter.

Liz pressed the doorbell, which triggered a familiar Christmas melody, "Santa Claus is Coming to Town." Within 30 seconds, Holly met her at the door.

"You made it," Holly said. "Come on in."

When Liz entered, she found herself facing the solid wall of a narrow hallway; she looked down the hall to her right and to her left. It was dim, with the only light coming from dirty exterior windows, and it was crowded with old chairs that she wouldn't want to sit on. Cobwebs draped from the ceiling to the floor.

The wall in front of her featured a heavy wooden door, with a security pad and large deadbolt lock. It was closed, and it looked as if it would take guile and super-human strength to open.

"Come on," Holly said. She punched in a code on the keypad, took a single key from around her neck and turned it in the lock.

Liz wondered about the double-door entrance. "Why do you have two back doors? This hallway makes the house look deserted."

Holly laughed. "Twirly says it's for privacy, keeping secrets, keeping the riffraff out and about 10 other things. Twirly likes to talk."

Liz followed Holly through the large door into the real interior of the Haints.

"This is where I live," Holly said.

It felt as different from the outer hallway as an amusement park does from a fifth-grade classroom. She stood in a large space with a high ceiling. On the wall to her left was a portrait of Santa Claus. Below the smiling figure with his big white beard and red nose was a long table filled with scale model Christmas village houses, adorned for the season with little yellow lights that shined through small windows. On the wall to her right was a mural of the North Pole, just as she'd always imagined it. It showed reindeer butting heads in a snowy field, happy elves at work on an assembly line, Mrs. Claus baking cookies in a comfortable kitchen and lots of wrapped presents. Liz felt her maturing brain tamping down feelings of when she was a young believer.

The centerpiece of the room was a fresh green Christmas tree that reached to the top of the 20-foot ceiling. An elderly man in a tweed jacket stood beside it, his hands clasped behind his back and a big smile on his face. Liz had never seen an older man with a ponytail.

"Welcome, Liz. Holly told me you were coming. My name is Twirly Masters, but you can call me Twirly. We are so delighted you could visit. Just delighted."

"Thank you for having me," Liz said. "It's really nice inside."

Twirly looked around. "Nothing like the outside, is it?" Twirly laughed. "But you can thank Holly for the inside. She's been doing her rotation on the house and grounds committee, and I must say, it's been a splendid improvement. Yes, splendid indeed."

"I thought I would show Liz around. May I show her the work spaces?" Holly asked.

"We have no secrets from Thad Raker's daughter," Twirly said.

Liz was surprised. "How do you know my dad?"

"Funny you should ask. I just got back from having lunch with him. He's my lawyer."

"Daddy is your lawyer? For what?"

"The county wants to take this property away from me and use it for a park. But if anyone can stop that from happening, it's your dad. So don't worry about me. I'm in good hands. Yes, good hands. You two run along and have fun. And Holly, remember what I said. The assignment I gave you is very important."

There was something about the house that begged to be explored, and Liz was happy to be invited to do it. In the first room, there was a ceiling-high Christmas tree, covered with popcorn strings and handmade decorations. In the next room, she saw another tree, this one more polished, draped with tinsel and bright shiny ornaments. In fact, each room had a tree with a different motif, with wreaths, garlands and lights. Each new one dazzled Liz more than the last.

Holly led her into the kitchen and she smelled cinnamon and sugar. A woman pulled a pie out of the oven as they approached.

"Well, hello there, Holly. Who is your friend?"

"This is Liz," Holly said. "Liz, this is Ms. Patten. She's our cook. And she's the best."

"That's very nice of you to say, Holly. And it's very nice to meet you, Liz. Would the two of you like a piece of pie?"

"Thanks," Holly said, "but I'm going to show Liz the work spaces."

Liz was a little disappointed. The aroma of the pie reminded her that she was hungry. But Holly walked on, took the key from around her neck and inserted it into a big lock in a narrow door. Liz heard voices on the other side and what sounded like laughter.

"It's break time," Holly said. "They're probably having a snack or playing games."

"Who?" Liz asked.

"The elves."

"What?"

"Yeah, I know. They take breaks all the time. I guess it's the union thing. They negotiated pretty hard for their snack and playtime."

Before Liz could ask another question, Holly opened the door to steps that descended to a basement. When she did, there was an explosion of joyful noise coming from below. When they arrived at the foot of the steps, Liz saw a room as large as the perimeter of the house, full of colorfully dressed people, all about Holly's height. They did look like elves, or at least what she imagined elves would look like if they existed. Some wore cone-shaped hats with little bells, and shoes that curled at the toes. Some wore skirts. Others wore pants with red suspenders. Some wore green vests. Many of them were gathered around a long table in one corner of the room, which was covered with fruits, nuts, cookies and candy. They were busy grabbing snacks and gobbling them down. Then the room got quiet and Liz realized everyone was looking at her.

"Everyone, this is my friend," Holly said.

A fellow with bright red hair and beady black eyes stepped out of the crowd and interrupted her.

"What are you doing bringing an outsider down here?"

"Chip," Holly said with authority in her voice, "Twirly said it's OK."

A polite girl spoke up. "What's your name, Holly's friend?"

"My name is Liz. Liz Raker."

"You're the lawyer's daughter, aren't you?" Chip asked. He didn't look happy.

Liz wondered how he could know that. "Yes. My dad is an attorney. His name is Thad Raker."

"Thought so," Chip said. "Another reason she shouldn't be here, Holly."

"And why is that?" Holly asked.

"Her dad can't keep secrets about our business, so why should she?"

"Don't pay attention to him," Holly said to Liz. "He's always complaining about something."

Just then a bell rang and the troop scattered around the room and through several doors. Someone must have flipped a switch, because conveyor belts that ran around and across the room came alive.

"Let me show you how it works," Holly said. She handed Liz some earplugs. "Union rules."

She pointed to one side of the room where a conveyor belt came through a square hole in the middle of the wall carrying packages. Raising her voice to be heard above the humming machinery, she said, "When presents arrive from up north, they're stored in our general collection area on the other side of that wall. Then they're loaded on the conveyor. When they come into this room, we sort them by the district where they need to be delivered, kind of like the post office does with letters that have ZIP codes. They then go into that room."

She led Liz through a double door into the area where the presents were being conveyed. This room was even bigger than the last.

"Your basement seems much larger than your house," Liz said.

"Four times as big," Holly said. "Stand back."

Liz moved just in time to avoid a forklift heading for the conveyor. It took a stack of boxes labeled District 4 off of one of the belts, did a U-turn and carried them away. Three other forklifts headed their way, all at full speed. Liz stepped back to avoid being run over, and adjusted the plugs in her ears. Holly tugged her arm to take her to a quieter spot.

"We stack the presents by district," Holly said, "and use different shelving to sort them within the district to make the deliveries faster."

"Who are the presents for?" Liz asked.

"They're for the believers, of course. Come on, there's more."

Holly picked up her pace, and Liz quickened her step to keep up. The next door they entered put them in a room with workbenches against all four walls. The people dressed as elves labored away under different signs, including ones that read Children's Toys, Games, Electronics and Clothing. They wore red work aprons with the letters "NPE" in green on the front.

"What's that?" Liz asked. She pointed at an electronic sign with a bright red number 18 on it.

"It's the number of days left until Christmas," Holly said.

Liz was trying to make sense of everything she had just seen when Holly interrupted her thoughts. "Twirly gave me an assignment this afternoon, and when he found out you were coming to visit, he said you can help, if you're willing. Would you help me?"

"Sure, what do we need to do?"

"We need to find a legal document. It's called a lease extension. Twirly is not sure where he put it, but if we don't find it before midnight on December 21st, the court will kick us out of the Haints."

"You mean you won't have a home for Christmas? That's sad."

"Sadder than you think," Holly said. "If we get kicked out, lots of children won't have Christmas at all. Then they won't believe anymore."

December 7ᵗʰ

7:45 p.m.

Liz sat with her schoolwork in front of her, but her head was swimming with the details of her visit to the Haints. She had too many questions. What did Holly mean when she said the presents were for the believers? Why did Holly call the workers "elves"? And why did they look like elves? And why was a toy company operating out of the basement of an old house? For that matter, why was there so much secrecy about what went on inside the house? It was like they were trying to hide what they were doing from the world.

Finally, she closed her books and went to find her dad. He was in his chair in the den, reading the newspaper. She sat on the couch beside Comet, and rubbed his head.

"Daddy," Liz asked, "have you ever been inside the Haints?"

Raker folded his paper and looked at her. "When we were kids, we used to go to the property, but we never went inside. We were too scared. We just threw rocks at it and dared ourselves to look in the windows. Why do you ask?"

"Do you remember the little girl I told you I met on my birthday, who thinks she works for Santa Claus?"

"You said something about her being an elf-in-training."

"Her name is Holly and she lives at the Haints. She gave me a tour today. I even met your client, Twirly Masters. He seems like a nice man."

"Rather talkative," Raker said, "but yes, he is a nice man. Tell me about the house."

"It's a house within a house. You can't tell until you get through the second door, but it's big and pretty, with Christmas trees everywhere. There also is a secret basement. And people everywhere, working like crazy, receiving, stacking and making gifts."

"Really? They make things there?" Raker said.

"There's more, Daddy. The people who live and work there dress in funny outfits and look like children, but like old children. It was strange."

"Did Twirly explain any of this to you?"

"No," Liz said, "But he did tell me that the county wants to take away his property and Holly said that if she and I can't find a thing called a lease extension, many children won't have Christmas. Is that possible?"

"On the day we met, Twirly hinted that winning the case and keeping the property would save Christmas, but I didn't take him seriously."

"This may sound like a stupid question," Liz said, "but do you think it's possible that Twirly and Holly actually *do* work for Santa Claus?"

"That's an odd question from someone who doesn't believe."

"I said I'm having a hard time believing. It's not the same thing as not believing. Besides, if you saw what I saw today, you would ask the same question. Has Twirly told you what they really do at the Haints?" she asked.

"He hasn't said and I haven't pushed him."

"Well, it doesn't matter. He shouldn't lose his property, especially at Christmas. It's not right." Liz was determined to help her dad save the Haints. "Holly and I will find that document, Daddy, I promise."

Liz got up and rubbed Comet's head. "Come on, Comet, time for you and me to go to bed. I need to rest up so I can help Daddy find an important document." Comet jumped down from the sofa and followed her as she left the room.

Raker reached for his wallet and found the contact card that Twirly Masters had given him the day they met. He wasn't sure he wanted to hear what Masters would tell him, because he didn't know if he would be able to believe it. As he dialed the number, he reminded himself to keep an open mind. He smiled at the thought that Elizabeth was looking down on him at this very moment to see how he did.

The phone rang only once before Masters answered. "Hello, Thad, and a very good evening to you. I presume you've been talking with Liz about her visit here today."

"She had some rather interesting stories to tell," Raker said. "I think it's about time you filled me in."

"I was hoping you would ask," Masters said. "Where should I start?"

"Let's try the beginning," Raker said. "That's usually a good place to start."

For the next 30 minutes, Masters talked and Raker listened, without interruption. When Masters finally finished, Raker's head was spinning and his heart hurt. He wished Elizabeth were with him. She would know what to do.

"Are you there, Thad?"

"I'm here," Raker said. "Just thinking."

"Was it too much, too fast?" Masters asked.

"No, I asked you to tell me everything. You did as I asked."

"So do you now understand why this case is so important?"

"Give me a chance to think about what you told me," Raker said. "In the meantime, find that lease extension."

December 14th

11:00 a.m.

Raker was in his office when his cell phone rang. "Thad, it's me, Sarah. If you don't have plans for lunch, I'd love to catch up. I also have something important to discuss about our case."

"How about the Knife and Fork at 12:15?"

"Sure. Shall I tell the maître d' we need a booth for two?"

For the next 45 minutes, Raker worked on his to-do list for the trial. At the top of the list was the lease extension. He knew Liz and Holly were looking for it, and it had to be somewhere, but so far, no luck. If they didn't find it, none of what he was working on would matter. There would be no need for a trial, because Twirly would be evicted. And even if they did find the lease extension, Twirly wouldn't be entitled to the full value of the property, only the value of the lease. But of course, that didn't matter either, because Twirly didn't care about the money. He was determined to prevent the condemnation of the property.

As Raker was thinking about these problems, his office phone rang. "Thad Raker."

"Hi, Raker. It's me, Austin Land, your friendly neighborhood trial reporter."

Raker saw Land around town on occasion, but hadn't spoken with him in years. It was true that Land's coverage of the Edmonds trial had been a big help in that case, but what he'd written about the Patten trial had only added to Raker's misery.

"What can I do for you, Mr. Land?"

"Call me Austin, but a better question is, what I can do for you?"

"Meaning what?" He felt his jaw clench. The reporter was as arrogant as ever, always seeming to take credit for his role in the "trial of the century."

"Meaning I have some information that might be helpful to you," Land said.

"Why would you share information with me?" Raker asked. "I thought reporters only ask for information."

"What I have learned may lead to an interesting courtroom story, but by itself, it is just one piece of the puzzle," Land said. "It concerns the case you're handling for Twirly Masters."

"What's the catch?"

"I give you what I know, keep you informed of what I learn along the way, and you give me an exclusive when the trial is over."

Raker wasn't sure about making any sort of arrangement with Land, but he needed help. "My client will have to be the one to decide whether to talk."

Land laughed. "I'll take that as a deal. I know enough about Twirly Masters to know he doesn't mind talking."

"OK, then. Be quick. I have a lunch appointment. What have you got?"

After his call with Austin Land, Raker walked across the street to the Knife and Fork and grabbed a table in the corner. The information Land had shared might indeed make a difference in the case. He was thinking about how he might use it when Sarah arrived. Before she took her seat, she leaned in to give him a quick light hug. Raker hesitated and Sarah noticed.

"Thad, I won't bite, even if we are on opposite sides in this case."

Raker tried to laugh but his nerves got the better of him. He knew it wasn't just the trial that made him hold back. Whether he wanted it to happen or not, he felt something move in his heart when he was close to her.

"Sorry, Sarah. I'm just a little distracted, trying to understand some things that don't make sense."

"Is it Liz again?"

"No, it's some things my client told me, although I do admit that on some days, I feel like filing a missing person report for a little girl I used to tuck in at night, because she's not so little anymore and doesn't need much of my help. Not with her homework. Not at bedtime. And the magic is disappearing; she stopped believing in Santa Claus."

Sarah put her right hand on Raker's left forearm and smiled. "Growing up is a natural part of life, for daughters and their dads."

"Maybe if I spent more time with her I could —"

"I saw Liz at Laura's house a few days ago, and she was chattering away about this case. Somehow, she found out about my involvement and was giving me a hard time about representing the bad guys. She is proud of you, as she should be. You have done a remarkable job raising her."

A strange combination of feelings surged through Raker. "Thanks. That's kind of you to say. It doesn't make Liz any younger, but it's kind of you to say." Raker started to tell Sarah he was worried that Liz would become too involved in the case and be disappointed if he lost. But he held back.

The waitress broke the mood by putting two glasses of water on the table and offering to take orders. When she was gone, Sarah turned serious.

"Thad," she said, "I have been tasked with bringing you a message from the county. Cleve figured you wouldn't meet with him, so he sent me. I wish I didn't have to do it, but it's my job. I hope you understand."

"I understand, and, believe me, you're the messenger I prefer."

"Thanks, I think." She laughed. "I will get straight to it. We know that Mr. Masters doesn't own the property. Even so, the county is prepared to settle by offering four times the tax value."

"Why in the world would the county offer that kind of money to a tenant?"

"I don't know," Sarah said. "But I do know the offer is a great deal for your client. He could do a lot with $400,000."

"There's one problem," he said. "Great deal or not, my client doesn't want the money."

"Has he told you why?" Sarah asked.

"He says the property has more value to the public just the way it is."

"Care to explain?"

"It's complicated," he said, "but I'll present the offer to him. I just know he won't take it. He's made it clear that money is not important to him."

Lunch arrived and they began to eat in silence.

"May I tell you something in confidence, Thad?" She put down her fork.

"Sure." He could tell from her tone of voice it was important, so he looked her in the eye.

"I've decided to leave the law firm, but I haven't told anyone yet."

"Good for you," he said. "It's about time."

"I'm going to look for a job in another state. I think I need a fresh start."

He reached for his water glass to cover the effect those words had on him.

"What do you think?" Sarah asked. "Would you miss me?" She smiled, but he heard her swallow an emotion.

"I won't miss you making Cleve R. Johnson look good in court, if that's what you're asking."

"That's not what I'm asking, Thad."

It must have seemed to Sarah like he was stalling. He was. He didn't know what to say, but he did know how he felt. There was no denying it now. He wanted her to stay. But before he could tell her, she let him off the hook. "Don't worry about it. I'll be sure to write."

After that, neither of them seemed to be very hungry and they let the waitress remove the half-eaten sandwiches from the table. Sarah had one piece of unfinished business to pass along. "There was one more thing Cleve wanted me to tell you."

"Go on."

"If you don't accept the offer, he's going to ask the court to evict Mr. Masters. The offer is good until midnight on the 21st, the first day of the trial. That is the day your client's lease expires."

"Seems like my client is in a difficult spot," Raker said.

"I agree. If he doesn't accept the offer, he might get nothing and have to vacate the property."

Raker didn't mention the lease extension, but he wondered if she knew anything about it. He also wondered if she knew why the county hadn't brought the owner of the property into the case. But he left that alone, because he knew the answer to that question. The call from Austin Land before lunch had supplied him with that information.

Raker called Masters on his way back to the office. "The county is offering you $400,000 for the property. That's a lot of money. Four times the tax value."

"There's still time, Thad. Holly and Liz are looking hard for the lease extension. They'll find it. Besides, I smell something fishy here. Dead fish. Somebody is up to no good. Absolutely no good. And just to be clear, I'm not settling this case for $400,000 or four times $400,000."

"OK, it's your call," Raker said. "But if they don't find the lease extension, you'll lose the property, along with the money for a replacement.

December 19ᵗʰ

11:00 a.m.

Judge Stark got out of his aging sedan and walked up the long sidewalk to the two-story home of Judge Ratliff Davidson. At the front door, he knocked twice.

"It's unlocked," a voice yelled from the other side.

Judge Stark opened the door to an unoccupied foyer. "In here."

Following the voice, Judge Stark entered a medium-sized den to find Judge Davidson in a comfortable chair, his leg in a cast and propped up on an ottoman. He started to try to rise.

"Keep your seat," Judge Stark said. "I may be the only active judge in this room, and wholly deserving of your respect, but I see you are in need of a sympathetic ruling."

Ratliff Davidson laughed. "Your one-month term on the bench is already going to your head, you old coot. Next thing you know, you'll be asking for your job back."

"It does have its perks," Judge Stark said. "I miss being in charge, which hasn't happened much in retirement with you-know-who."

"I always said, your Kay truly was the match for you, but of course, she's more sensible, patient and understanding." Ratliff laughed again.

In response, Judge Stark tossed a rubber-banded stack of letters at the man. "Your courthouse mail. My errand is complete."

After eyeing a few of the return addresses on the envelopes, Ratliff said, "So tell me. What have I been missing? Anything interesting?"

"You would think the criminals would be getting smarter, but I don't see it. Dumb as ever."

"What about the civil cases?" Ratliff asked.

"Most are routine, but I do have one that might interest you. The trial starts on Monday." For the next five minutes, Judge Stark shared what little he knew about the county's case to condemn the property owned by Twirly Masters.

"So Raker's involved, huh?" Ratliff asked.

"He is, and I think he has his hands full this time. The county has spared no expense on the legal team. It must really want the property."

"You know," Ratliff said, "I had a case with Raker once. It was during the summer about seven years ago, but the events took place on Christmas Eve. It involved a woman named Gloria Patten."

"Was that the one with the woman who claimed she was attacked by flying Christmas presents?"

"That's the one. After Raker saved Christmas in your courtroom, he fell on his holiday-loving face in mine. But the interesting thing is this. His client didn't sound crazy to me. Sure, her story sounded like something out of a science-fiction movie, but she had a good memory of what occurred, nice attention to detail and a spotless character."

"So why do you think she lost the case?"

"No evidence. The highway patrol was on the scene in 30 minutes but saw nothing that would have caused her car to veer off the road except operator error."

"Sounds pretty open and shut to me," Judge Stark said.

"Yes, but now that Raker is in your courtroom again, I should tell you a few things that may be helpful."

"Go on."

"During the Patten trial, a short man sat in the back of the courtroom, watching. He was there for the entire trial. I'm pretty sure he's the same man who barged into your courtroom and made trouble for Raker in the Edmonds trial."

"I know who you're talking about," Judge Stark said.

"Well, here's the thing," Ratliff said. "That man came to both of Raker's Christmas-themed trials, right? Why would he have any interest in a motor-vehicle negligence case involving a Christmas Eve accident, unless..."

"Unless what?"

"Well, unless he was involved somehow and there was some truth to Ms. Patten's story about flying presents."

Judge Stark thought the idea of flying presents was nothing more than a creative but frivolous defense that failed, but he remained silent.

"That case always nagged at me," Ratliff said, "so I poked around on the Internet to learn about small flying machines."

"What did you learn?" Judge Stark was just keeping his friend company.

"It turns out, drones are all the commercial rage. Did you know that major online retailers are taking the idea of using drones to make deliveries quite seriously, and have been experimenting? There are limitations as to how much weight an average-sized drone can carry, and how far it can fly before its batteries need recharging. There are safety issues, too, including the reliability of onboard GPS directional systems, and how they deposit their packages without causing harm to persons or property. The economics of the whole thing also is under debate, but there are pluses. They don't require a pilot, and they won't get caught in traffic."

"So what have you concluded about the accident from your research?"

"I think it's possible that Ms. Patten was faced with a sudden emergency and it was caused by drones carrying Christmas presents. Maybe the drones powered down and the presents came unlatched and fell from the sky. Or maybe the drones just malfunctioned and drove themselves and the presents into the ground."

Judge Stark leaned forward. It was time to push back. "It sounds pretty tenuous to me. If you're right, why wasn't there any evidence of wreckage at the accident scene?"

"I've asked myself that question and more," Ratliff said. "But I can't get over the feeling that there's something to it. Don't you think it's suspicious that the same man who made trouble in your courtroom was in the back of mine when the verdict came down against Ms. Patten?"

"He said he worked for an international toy company," Judge Stark said.

"There you go," Ratliff said. "It all fits. His toy company must have developed a program to deliver presents with drones."

"I don't know," Judge Stark said.

"Look, Augustus, odds are the man's involved. So you tell me. Does he work for an international toy company, or..." Ratliff smiled. "Or, was Edmonds right about who the man really works for?"

Judge Stark scoffed. "Those pain pills you're taking must have messed with your head." He got up. "I've got to go. Leave you to your fantasies."

Ratliff laughed again. "Now remember what I've said, old friend. And remember this. You can't discount the truth just because it appears far-fetched."

Lease Extension

90 Acres off Highway 11

Chief Operating Officer,
North Pole Enterprises

December 21ˢᵗ

9:30 a.m.

Raker showed up early in courtroom 4112 for the beginning of the 10:00 o'clock trial. He groaned when he saw Cleve R. Johnson's technical team wiring the courtroom so the county lawyers could amaze the jury with electronic visual aids. Not only would it make for a more efficient presentation, but it would entertain the jurors. Make it like watching television. Raker couldn't afford the bells and whistles, no matter how effective.

Cleve R. Johnson arrived at 9:59, and the judge entered precisely at 10:00. Raker caught Judge

Stark's frown when he saw Johnson was in place. Maybe the judge was hoping to add to his watch collection.

"Is everyone ready to proceed?" Judge Stark asked.

"If it please the court," Johnson said.

"Go ahead."

"I would be remiss if I didn't give the court notice of an important fact in the case," Johnson said. "Mr. Masters is only a tenant on the property."

"Why are you waiting until now to tell me about this? Where is the owner and why isn't the owner a party in this case?" Judge Stark asked.

"The county has an agreement with the owner. It's the tenant, Mr. Masters, who is the problem." Johnson was on a roll. "In addition — and this is very important — his lease expires today."

"Excuse me?" Judge Stark said.

"That's right." Johnson was pleased with himself. "At midnight, Mr. Raker's case will disappear, just like his defense did in the Patten case. Now that was a classic."

Judge Stark sat up straight. "Mr. Johnson, why have you been wasting the court's time on this condemnation case if the county has an agreement with the owner and the tenant's lease is about to expire?"

"My client initially thought there was a lease extension, but as of today, no record of it has been filed with the Register of Deeds. In the morning, we plan to file a motion to dismiss this case and evict Mr. Masters."

Judge Stark turned to Raker. "Mr. Raker, is it true what Mr. Johnson said about the lease?"

Raker felt all eyes were on him. "Yes, sir, it is."

"And you want to proceed anyway?"

"Yes, sir. My client has a leasehold interest in the property, which allows him to challenge the county's right to take the property. If the court allows the taking, he has the right to be compensated."

"That may be accurate," Judge Stark said, "but those rights only extend as long as the lease."

"My client has a written lease extension," Raker said. "We hope to produce it for the court very soon."

"You hope? Not good enough. If I don't have the lease extension when court opens in the morning, we will take up the motion to dismiss and evict. It is not something I look forward to ruling on this close to Christmas, but I will do my duty."

Cleve R. Johnson bowed from the waist. "We appreciate that, your honor."

"Mr. Johnson. Despite what you may think, I am not doing this for you. It's time to pick a jury. We should have enough time to get it done today."

As Raker sat down, he glanced across the aisle. The bastion of litigators who surrounded Cleve R. Johnson was buoyant, with the exception of Sarah Kennedy. She met Raker's eyes and gave him a sad shrug as if to say, sorry.

December 21ˢᵗ

2:00 p.m.

Holly and Liz had looked for the lease extension every weekday afternoon for the past two weeks. This morning, they had started early, because it was the first day of Liz's Christmas break. They had gone through three rooms they had searched previously: the attic, the basement, and the chaotic room Twirly called his office. Once again, they had no luck.

"I don't think it's in the house," Liz said. "Is there any place else to search?"

Holly nodded. "There are two buildings on the property."

"Lead the way," Liz said.

As they left the back of the house, the land fell off to a pasture below. In the distance, Liz saw a small building connected to a one-acre fenced area. "Is that where we're headed?" she asked.

"Yes, we'll look there first. It's the reindeer paddock."

"What do you mean, the reindeer paddock?"

"Santa stops his sleigh there on Christmas Eve for the reindeer to rest up."

"OK, then, let's try the reindeer paddock." Liz had gotten used to Holly's fantasies.

Liz stepped into a building that looked the way a barn should look, with stalls and feed bins. It smelled like fresh straw and leather, too, but it had something she didn't expect: a big room behind the stalls that was full of filing cabinets. They both got excited.

"I think this is it," Liz said.

"You're right, but Twirly definitely keeps too much paper. That's why I want to work in the records department when I become a fully certified, mature elf, so I can digitize all this stuff. Plus, I want to work with The Archives."

"What're The Archives?" Liz asked.

"It's where we keep a record of all the children and all the presents they received from Santa Claus until they stop believing. It's also where we keep track of the True Believers, the adults who find it within themselves to believe again."

"You mean there's a record on me, and all the presents I received?" Liz asked.

"Sure is."

"How do you know?"

"I'm a trainee. I see these things. How else would I know that you received an E-reader for Christmas last year?"

"Lucky guess, maybe, because you know I like to read," Liz said.

Holly laughed. "You'll come around. Just stay close to me."

After three hours of digging through the cabinets, they were dejected once again.

"It's not here," Liz said. "We're running out of time."

"There's only one other place to look, a storage building on the other side of the pasture. Let's go." Holly took off running, Liz right behind her.

They hadn't gone far before Holly tripped and fell over something. Liz reached down to pick her up and saw what had caused the fall: a red object partially buried in the ground, as if it had fallen from the sky and plunged halfway into the earth. Liz tried to pull it up, but it was stuck fast. Bending down on one knee, she turned her head and read an exposed inscription in the corner.

"It says Vesta. Do you know what that means, Holly?"

"No idea." Holly got up and brushed herself off. "We don't have time for it, whatever it is. Let's hurry."

They arrived at the building out of breath. "This place is huge," Liz said. "It's like a big box store." She followed Holly in and down a hallway lined with doors, all closed.

"Look at the sign on this one," Liz said. "Important documents." They both laughed.

"This has to be it," Holly said. She pushed the door open and they looked in.

Their hearts sank. The room was long and wide and had file cabinets along all four walls, and more in a square in the center.

"We can't stand around," Liz said. "I'll start over here. You take the ones in the middle of the room."

Liz worked her way through several cabinets on one wall until she came to one labeled "Legal." Her initial optimism gave way to disappointment when she realized it was stuffed full of newspaper articles about lawsuits from around the world. Then a name caught her eye. It was an article about a trial involving Gloria Patten, the pie-baker she'd met at the Haints. Her dad's name was there, too. She hesitated, but then did a quick read. The criticism in the article made her even more determined to help her dad.

Liz picked up her pace, continuing along the first wall of cabinets. When she turned the corner, she noticed an interesting sign above the cabinets. "The cabinets on this wall are full of Christmas songs," she said.

Holly gasped and ran to her. "I have an idea. A few nights ago, Ms. Patten told me how Twirly reacted when he received the lease extension. She said there was a man who works for Santa Claus who didn't want Twirly to get the extension, and Santa Claus overruled him. Twirly was so happy with the extension, he didn't stop singing his favorite Christmas song for the next two weeks. She said he put great emphasis on the portion of the song where everyone is laughing all the way."

"'Jingle Bells,'" Liz said. She turned back to the Christmas-song cabinets and looked for the 4-drawer cabinet with the letter "J" at the top.

"Maybe we've finally figured out how to think like Twirly," she said. She went through the "J" cabinet drawers until she found the file she wanted. "Here it is, the 'Jingle Bells' file." She opened it, looked inside, and there it was, a document titled "Lease Extension" in big bold letters across the top. Holly joined her and they read it together.

"This will make my dad really happy," Liz said.

"And Twirly will laugh his head off," Holly added. "He should be out of court. I'll text him." But before she could, the door opened and in walked the beady-eyed Chip, followed by a man Liz didn't know. He stood only 3 feet tall. He was well-dressed in a black suit and a red tie decorated with green Christmas trees. His eyes were black as coal, and he made Liz nervous.

"So you found it, did you?" Chip said.

"What do you want, Chip?" Holly stood in front of Liz ready to fight to protect their find. As Chip took a step closer, Liz noticed Holly blinking her eyes and snapping the fingers on her right hand, touching Liz's shoulder with her left.

"It won't work, Holly," Chip said. "You don't have your powers yet. Just a trainee, remember? There will be no disappearing act for you and your friend." He pointed at the man. "This gentleman is Mr. Hank Snow. He is a senior officer of the company that owns this property. He wants to speak with you."

"Thank you, Chip," Snow said. He turned to face Liz and Holly. "Children, I need to take a look at the document you found. I need to be sure it's genuine."

Liz didn't trust the man. She shook her head as she put the lease extension behind her back.

"Just a quick look," Snow said. "What harm can there be in that?"

Liz wished her dad was there to tell her what to do, but she was on her own.

"As long as you just look," she said. She held it out so that he could see the front page, but she kept hold of it. To her surprise, he reached over and grabbed it.

"Wait," she said.

"You can't do that," Holly said.

"You girls did a fine job." Snow folded the document, put it in his coat pocket and walked out the door.

Liz and Holly charged after him, but Chip pushed them back and blocked their way. He was bigger and stronger but that didn't stop Holly from jumping on his back and pulling him away to open space for Liz to get through the door. She ran down the long hallway as quickly as she could, through the front door and onto the porch. By the time she got there, Snow was kneeling over a small fire in the front yard. Liz felt her stomach lurch; the lease extension was going up in flames.

Holly and Chip appeared behind her.

"I've called Twirly for help," Holly said.

But it was too late. Chip ran over to Snow and they strolled off, a pile of fading embers on the ground.

Twirly was there in ten minutes. "Are you two OK?" he asked. "Holly, you made it sound more urgent than a five-alarm fire!"

"We found the lease extension," Holly said, "but Chip must have followed us, and he brought that Mr. Snow with him. They destroyed it." She pointed to the ashes.

"A fire, indeed," Twirly said. "And a very big one at that."

"We need to tell my dad what happened," Liz said.

Raker was on his front porch tossing a ball to Comet to relieve his anxiety while he waited. Twirly had called to say Liz was upset about something and they were on their way. He hadn't explained the problem; as usual, it was difficult to get a straight answer from him. Finally, Twirly's car pulled up and Liz jumped out and ran to him. He held out his arms for her, but Comet intercepted the connection and jumped at her. She kneeled down and buried her head in his fur, rubbing his ears. It didn't hide the fact that she had been crying.

"Liz, what's wrong?" Raker asked. "Are you hurt?"

"No," Liz said. "I'm not hurt, but I failed." She went over and put her arms around Raker's waist and leaned into him.

Then Holly blurted out, "It was Hank Snow. He stole the lease extension from us."

"And he burned it," Liz added, wiping her eyes.

"Let's go inside," Raker said. He held his daughter's hand, his heart breaking for her, his lawyer's brain considering the problem for his client. When everyone found a seat, with Comet at Liz's feet, Liz and Holly told the story about how they searched for the lease extension, found it and then lost it to Hank Snow.

"Daddy, you're always so sad at Christmastime. I knew that if I could find the lease extension, you would win the case and be happy this year. I'm sorry I let you down."

"It's not your fault, Liz. I'm very proud of you, and Holly, too. It was brave of you to stand up to Hank Snow."

"It certainly was," Twirly said. "You two had courage. Yes, indeed!"

Raker heard someone knock on the front door and a voice called, "Is anyone home?" Comet jumped down and ran to the door, barking at the intruder.

"That's Ms. Sarah," Liz said. "We should tell her about Hank Snow."

"I should probably speak with her alone," Raker said. He got up, told Comet everything was fine and met Sarah Kennedy on the porch, pulling the front door shut behind him.

"I'm sorry," she said. "Am I interrupting something?"

"Liz had a shock at the Haints today," he said.

"Oh, that's awful, can I see her?"

"Thanks, but we'd better not, because Twirly Masters is here with us. I will let her know you asked about her. She'll be fine."

Sarah looked down and hesitated. Raker didn't think he'd ever seen her so ill at ease. "What is it, Sarah?"

"You probably think I've made a deal with the devil," she said. "This was supposed to be a simple condemnation case. I didn't know you were involved until after I was committed to the case, and now Liz is involved."

"It's not your fault."

Sarah looked Raker in the eye. "I'm here to plead with you to take the $400,000 offer. My boss tells me he's sure that the lease extension can't be produced. I don't know how he knows that, and I don't think I want to know. But he says the county's offer is still on the table."

"That's interesting," Raker said. "If Cleve knows he has a winner, it makes no sense for him to encourage the county to make this offer. I wonder if he's concerned about something coming out in the trial."

"I have no idea, Thad, but there won't be a trial if you can't produce the lease extension." Raker saw in her eyes that she was miserable; it just added to his sense of failure on the one hand and his regard for her on the other. He watched her get into her car and drive away.

As he walked back in the house, Raker thought about Hank Snow. It was during his cross-examination of Snow in the Edmonds trial that he reconnected with his youthful belief in Santa Claus and became a True Believer, but Elizabeth's death and the loss in the Patten trial had frayed his belief system. And now Snow was back. Why? And what did it mean for the case? More importantly, what did it mean about what he should believe?

Raker asked Twirly to come to the kitchen, so he could deliver Sarah's message. "Despite what happened to the lease extension, the $400,000 offer to settle is still available. If you take it, you can buy another property to do your work."

"Not in time to save Christmas. No, sir, not in time," Masters said. "I won't give in to Snow. They can keep their money."

"That's your final decision?" Raker asked. "If it is, you have a lot more faith in me than I have in myself. Without the lease extension, I'm out of arguments." He saw that Liz and Holly had come into the room.

"I warned Santa Claus that Snow would threaten Christmas again. Told him it was just a matter of time. Yes, I did. I sure did. Just a matter of time," Masters said.

"But Daddy," Liz said. "Can't you think of something? Without the lease extension, the Haints will be shut down."

Raker looked at Twirly. "Will you have a big problem this Christmas if we lose?"

"We manage the entire distribution system for Zone 24," Twirly said. "If we lose this case, the presents won't be delivered in the 30 districts in our zone, and hundreds of thousands of children will cease to believe in Santa Claus. Is that a big enough problem?"

December 22ⁿᵈ

9:30 a.m

As Raker entered the courtroom, Twirly was waiting for him. "Good morning, Thad. Hope you got a good night's sleep. Big day!"

"How do you stay so positive, Twirly?" Raker asked.

"Every day is a new day. And I'm grateful for that opportunity when I wake up. I try to live in the present. Yes, that's what I try to do. And that's about all there is to it. Sums it up pretty well."

"But the lease extension is gone. I thought you would be depressed," Raker said.

"Thad, I don't have time to be depressed. There are too many things to do and too many children to think about with Christmas fast approaching. At this time of year, you could rain on my parade from sunup to sundown and I wouldn't be depressed. It's such a wonderful season."

"Will you feel that way when you get evicted from the property today?"

"With a lawyer like you at my side, I have no worries about being evicted. Plus, I made a call last night to a good friend. I have a feeling things may work out just yet. And here are our most valuable helpers."

Raker looked around and saw Liz and Holly come into the courtroom. Liz waved and they found seats on the first row behind Raker and Masters. The county's legal team began to fill their space. Raker couldn't help but notice that Sarah Kennedy was the next-to-last of them to appear, followed by Johnson, with 30 seconds to spare. The bailiff opened court and Judge Stark walked up to the bench; he wasted no time.

"Mr. Raker, do you have the lease extension?"

Raker stood up. He had come to the conclusion that it would be hard to convince Judge Stark that Hank Snow burned the lease extension, and he didn't want to put Liz and Holly on the stand and subject them to Johnson's wrath. Even if the judge wanted to believe what Snow had done, there was no document to put into evidence.

"We don't have it, your honor."

Raker sat down and dropped into a semi-trance as Johnson began to argue for the dismissal of the lawsuit and the eviction of Twirly Masters. He approached the bench and handed a thick stack of papers to the judge. Judge Stark set them on a corner of his desk and gave them a hard look, almost as if they were responsible for what he was about to be required to do. Johnson said the motion included an affidavit from a representative of North Pole Enterprises authorizing the gift of the land to the county. Johnson handed Raker a copy of the affidavit; the name jumped off the page: Hank Snow.

When Johnson sat down, looking confident about the outcome of his motion, Raker noticed that Sarah was disturbed. She was looking down and shaking her head.

"Mr. Raker," Judge Stark said. "Mr. Johnson has made a compelling argument for the dismissal of this case and the eviction of your client. Do you have any response?"

As Raker was about to admit defeat, the judge's gaze shifted from him to the back of the courtroom, and his eyes widened. Raker turned to see for himself. A man had entered and stood in front of the main door. He was close to 6 feet 6 inches tall, and likely tipped the scales at around 275 pounds. His face was covered with salt-and-pepper stubble, and he had long white hair that fell to his shoulders. Raker felt dizzy. He thought of the bedtime story he had told his little girl when she was 4 years old. He thought of his little girl's full name: Elizabeth Henry Raker. He thought of her middle name: Henry. And there he stood. Liz's middle-name namesake, Henry Edmonds, was standing in the middle of the courtroom aisle.

"Mr. Raker," Judge Stark asked. "Is this man one of your witnesses?"

"Yes, your honor," Raker replied, improvising. He figured that if Henry was here, he must have come to help. "May we have five minutes, your honor?"

The judge frowned but looked again toward Henry Edmonds, and relented. "I suppose it won't hurt to give you a few minutes. We'll be at ease while the two of you talk."

Raker walked to the back of the courtroom where Edmonds was standing. "Hello, Henry." They shook hands. "You sure can pick your moment. We should probably talk in the hallway."

Raker escorted Henry from the courtroom and found a quiet corner for them to talk. There had been days when he felt sure Henry was gone for good, possibly dead. Other days he recanted. Of course Henry was alive, he would say to himself; he's immortal. And yet, the question had haunted him since that Christmas Eve 12 years earlier when Edmonds stood on a street corner in a Santa suit, wished him a very Merry Christmas and disappeared. Never to be heard from again. That is, until now.

"I'm sorry," Henry said. "After the trial, I was ordered to become invisible to the real world, including you. It was the price of keeping my job. I revealed too much in the trial."

"So, why now? Why are you back?" Raker asked.

"You helped me when I was on trial. I want to return the favor."

"You want to help me?" Raker asked.

"And save Christmas."

Raker dared to feel hopeful. "Do you have a copy of the lease extension?"

"No. But I have something better: I have a deed."

Raker grabbed Henry by the arm and hustled him back into the courtroom. Twirly sat at counsel table, waiting. Judge Stark was behind his bench, waiting. It seemed that everyone present was waiting, curious to know if Raker had learned anything important in his conversation with Henry Edmonds.

Judge Stark banged his gavel to tamp down the whispers. "Mr. Raker, I believe the floor is yours."

"Your honor," Raker said, "I don't have the lease extension, but I do have a document I would like to present to the court that will keep this trial on track."

"Come forward."

Raker approached the bench and handed the judge a rolled-up scroll tied in green and red string. Judge Stark took it, and as he did, he looked beyond Raker at Henry Edmonds. "Can Mr. Edmonds authenticate this document?"

"Yes, sir. I see that you remember him from the trial 12 years ago."

"You mean the 'trial of the century,' don't you? Nice to see you again, Mr. Edmonds," Judge Stark said. Raker was relieved to hear the judge's voice tinged with good humor.

Johnson was on his feet again. "Your honor, if this isn't the lease extension, I fail to see how a piece of paper is going to save this case."

"Well, let's take a look, shall we?" He untied the string and unwound a scroll that was twice as long as it was wide. After studying it for a moment, Judge Stark said, "It seems that North Pole Enterprises has deeded the property to Mr. Masters."

"That can't be possible," Johnson said. "I have an affidavit from Hank Snow authorizing the eviction of Mr. Masters. Snow is chief operating officer of that company."

"Mr. Johnson," Judge Stark said, "who has more authority, the chief operating officer or the president?" He held the deed up to the light. Even from where Raker was sitting, it revealed a watermark of a sleigh being pulled by eight tiny reindeer.

"I suppose the president has more power," Johnson said.

"This deed is signed by the president."

Just then, the main door of the courtroom swung open again. "Hank Snow," Judge Stark said. "I was wondering when you were going to interrupt the proceedings in my courtroom. Just like old times. Do you have something to say about this deed?"

"It has to be a forgery. I didn't authorize it."

Raker re-entered the conversation. "May we present Mr. Edmonds to authenticate the document, your honor?"

"By all means," Judge Stark replied. "We have a circus going on right now. Might as well make it a three-ring. I presume we don't need the jury for this."

"No, sir," Raker said, "we're satisfied to have you decide the issue." Johnson agreed, and Edmonds came up, took the witness chair and was sworn to tell the truth.

"Mr. Edmonds, is the deed authentic?" Raker asked.

"It is."

"So you are familiar with the president's signature?"

"I am. I've seen him sign his name hundreds of times. I have no doubt that the signature on this document is his."

Raker looked at the judge. "That's all, your honor, unless you have any questions of Mr. Edmonds about the document."

"Not at this time. I'll give Mr. Johnson his turn. I can see he is anxious to have it."

"Mr. Edmonds," Johnson started. "The last time you were in this courthouse, you were on trial for stealing a flash drive and assaulting a woman, correct?"

"Yes, but —"

Johnson cut him off. "No buts, Mr. Edmonds. Isn't it also true you are under the delusion that you work for Santa Claus?"

"No," Edmonds said. "I am under no delusion. I do work for Santa Claus."

Johnson raised his voice as he addressed Judge Stark with his hands in the air. "What an insult to the court system, your honor. This man is either lying or he's insane. He shouldn't be allowed to authenticate his own driver's license. The court should strike his entire testimony."

Judge Stark leaned back in his chair with the deed in his hand and rubbed his chin. After about 10 seconds of silence, he sat up and looked straight at Johnson. "As you may recall, Mr. Johnson, I was the judge who dismissed the case against Mr. Edmonds even though he testified he works for Santa Claus."

Without hesitating, Judge Stark swiveled his chair toward Edmonds. "Mr. Edmonds, you said you have no doubt that the signature on this deed is that of the president of North Pole Enterprises? Why is that?"

"Because," Edmonds said, "I saw him sign the deed last night."

Home run, Raker thought, as Twirly clapped his hands together in delight. He heard excited conversation between Liz and Holly, and turned around to motion for them to remain quiet. When he did, he saw reporter Austin Land pecking away furiously on his laptop. Turning back to face the judge, Raker noticed that Johnson's crew of lawyers was abuzz, except one, the woman on the team he held in high regard. She had a slight grin on her face.

Judge Stark looked back at Johnson. "I believe they call that checkmate, Mr. Johnson."

Johnson, who was bug-eyed in astonishment, wanted another shot at Henry Edmonds, so for the next five minutes, he launched into a full frontal assault on the man. He peppered him with question after question, and cut him off more than once.

Judge Stark finally had enough. "Mr. Johnson, earlier this month, I reminded you of my rules of court. Rule 3 requires lawyers to be courteous, even to those they don't like or believe. If you can't get a handle on your emotions, you will spend the night in a jail cell. I will let you have one last question. Be nice."

Johnson made a show of smoothing his suit jacket and straightening his tie.

"So tell us," he asked Edmonds, "other than your word, do you have any real proof that the signature of the president of North Pole Enterprises is authentic?"

"As a matter of fact I do. It's in the stack of papers right there." He pointed to the documents on the corner of Judge Stark's bench.

"For the record," Judge Stark said, "the witness is pointing to the motion to dismiss and evict presented by Mr. Johnson. Mr. Edmonds, can you show us?"

He handed the stack to Edmonds, who flipped through it and found the page he wanted. He held his finger on the page as he handed it back to Judge Stark, who took it and looked it over. "The witness has directed the court's attention to the signature page on the 45-year lease the county filed in support of its motion to dismiss and evict."

Looking at Mr. Johnson, Judge Stark asked: "Mr. Johnson, is the lease attached to your motion a true and accurate copy of the lease between Mr. Masters and North Pole Enterprises, LLC?"

Johnson said "yes," which led Judge Stark to pull the signature page of the lease out of the stack and lay it side by side with the deed. Raker thought he detected a slight grin on Judge Stark's face when he compared the two documents.

"Let the record show that the signatures of the president on these two documents match perfectly." He peered over his glasses and focused in Johnson's direction. "It's the ruling of the court that the motion to dismiss and evict is denied. The deed is legally binding. Mr. Masters is going to get his day in court after all. We'll start with the jury after lunch."

As the courtroom began to empty, Liz watched Henry Edmonds. She had so many questions for him, but she wasn't sure how to ask them. She watched him as he stepped down from the witness stand and walked toward counsel table. She continued watching as he spoke with her dad and then with Twirly Masters. When he left the counsel table and started walking down the aisle, she continued to keep her eyes on him, right up until the time he greeted her.

"Hello, Liz," Edmonds said. "It's very nice to meet you, finally."

"Nice to meet you, too," Liz said.

"My, oh my," Edmonds said, "you do have your mother's eyes."

"Did you know my mother for a long time?" Liz asked.

"Long enough to know how special she was and how lucky your dad was to marry her. I was best man at the wedding."

"But why did you stay away for so long? I'm named after you and you never came to see me. I don't even know you."

"That is something I regret the most about my absence these last 12 years," Edmonds said. "I wish I had been there to be a part of your life."

"Well, you weren't," Liz said. She crossed her arms and looked down.

"I know. An apology is not enough," Edmonds said. "It wasn't right for me to stay away, so I have to make it up to you."

"And how do you plan to do that?" She looked up at him but didn't uncross her arms.

"First, I'm going to be here to help support your dad through this trial. Second, I'm going to be the godfather I should have been and be there for you when you need me. Just ask, and I will do my best to help. Oh, and finally, if you're a believer when Christmas gets here in two days, I have some pull in the Christmas wish department."

"I suppose it doesn't hurt to have you on my side at this time of year." She tried to stay serious.

"I like the way you think, Liz. An analytical mind, just like your father."

December 22ⁿᵈ

2:00 p.m.

Judge Stark ordered the bailiff to bring in the jurors. He had run a tight ship during jury selection; he didn't allow the lawyers to pander to the venire. When Cleve R. Johnson tried to get to know the entire panel on a first-name basis, Judge Stark asked him whether he was trying to impanel a jury or looking for a new best friend. Raker had taken the judge's hint and kept to the basics. He was as satisfied as he could be with the result, because there was no way he could find a jury of one's peers for a man like Twirly Masters.

The audience was small. Raker and Twirly had their supporters in Henry, Laura, Liz and Holly, and the county's interests were backed by the county manager, the county commission chairman, and Hank Snow. Austin Land was set up in the back row on Twirly's side of the courtroom, his laptop at the ready.

With Christmas less than three days away, and at the strong-arm urging of Judge Stark, both sides agreed to waive opening statements and get on with the evidence. Cleve R. Johnson called his first witness, real estate appraiser Lori Lannigan. After the swearing-in and state-your-name routine, Johnson got right to work. He built up the witness by asking her to state her credentials. Yes, she was a board-certified appraiser. Yes, she was a member of the National Association of Appraisers. Yes, she had the MAI designation from the Appraisal Institute in Chicago. What did that mean? It meant she had the highest designation the esteemed institute could confer. How many years had she been doing appraisals? Thirty-five years. Education? A little school called Harvard. Post-graduate work? Yes, two masters degrees, one in business adminis-tration, and the other in urban planning. Lannigan told it all in a pleasant, professional tone.

After the royal treatment had been laid at the feet of Lori Lannigan, Johnson offered the witness to the court as an expert in the field of real estate appraisal. Judge Stark had to agree, and the crown was officially placed on Lannigan's head. Raker knew the jury was impressed. They were waiting for Lannigan to tell them how to vote.

Johnson moved to the topic at hand, prompting Lannigan to explain that at the county's request, she had conducted an appraisal of the subject property. Was it done by the book? Yes. Did she follow all protocols? Yes. Did she write a report? Of course. Did she have it with her? She sure did.

One of Johnson's associates punched a button and the first page of the appraisal appeared on the courtroom monitors. The associate worked the controls, going from one page to the next, as Johnson and Lannigan walked the jury and the judge through the appraisal. Some of the pages had pictures. There were ground level shots and a few satellite photos. There was a picture of the house, a decrepit looking structure. There was a plat and sketch, showing the size of the property and the locations of the house and two buildings. At the back of the document was the appraiser's standard certification page. It was boilerplate language but

Johnson made the words sound worthy of space alongside the Ten Commandments. The page covered such things as impartiality and adherence to strict ethical standards. Did Lannigan comply with all of the requirements, he asked. Of course she had.

Then Johnson asked the question Raker expected. "Do you have an opinion satisfactory to yourself, based on your extensive experience in the field of real estate appraisal and your examination and study of this and comparable properties, of the fair market value of the property owned by Mr. Twirly Masters?"

"I do," Lannigan said.

"Please share this information with the jury." Johnson had deftly shifted from calling it "opinion" to calling it "information." He made it sound like just another fact in the case. Raker knew what was coming: a number far lower than what Twirly could get for the property if he settled.

"The property has a total fair market value of $100,000," Lannigan said. Raker noticed that most of the jurors were making a note of that number on their notepads.

"How does that break down?" Johnson asked.

"The acreage has a fair market value of $90,000,

which is $1,000 an acre. The house is a tear-down; it has no value. One of the buildings, which appears to be used for storage, needs roof repairs that exceed the value of the building; thus, I give it no value. The other building is a well-maintained stable, valued at $10,000."

"Those are all my questions," Johnson said. Before he sat down, he looked around as if expecting applause from the judge and jury.

"Good morning, Ms. Lannigan." Raker was compliant with Judge Stark's Rule 3: Be courteous.

"Good morning, sir."

"Would you say that 75 percent of the condemnation cases you have handled in your 35 years of real estate appraisal work have been for local governments?"

"I don't know the exact percentage," Lannigan offered, "but that's pretty close. I have been fortunate to have repeat business and good recommendations from satisfied clients."

"Speaking of repeat business," Raker said. "You are on speed-dial with the county, are you not?"

"Excuse me?"

"They know how to find you quickly," Raker pressed.

"I suppose."

"Didn't you do a rush job for the county on Mr. Masters' property?" Raker asked.

"I was very careful," Lannigan replied.

"Let me rephrase the question. You didn't get this assignment until one week ago, did you?"

"That's correct."

"Aren't you usually given more notice than that?" Raker asked.

"I was able to work it in," Lannigan said.

"Is that because the county is a good client who pays well and on time?"

"I try to look after all my clients. When they have a need, I do my best to help."

"And in this case," Raker offered, "when the county told you it had a need to take my client's property, and it needed a fast appraisal, you were more than willing to drop everything and help."

"I was just doing my job, Mr. Raker."

Raker decided to go in a different direction. "Do you have a nickname, Ms. Lannigan?"

Johnson complained with vigor. "That question calls for an answer that is immaterial, irrelevant and a waste of the court's time. What next? Will Mr. Raker be asking Ms. Lannigan to map out her family tree?"

Raker couldn't have been more pleased with Johnson drawing attention to the question. He noticed that Sarah shook her head at Johnson's gaff. But Cleve R. Johnson, Esquire, couldn't help himself. If the script didn't go exactly as he planned, he would blow like a whale in distress. After Judge Stark overruled the objection, Raker prompted Lannigan again.

"Did you understand my question, Ms. Lannigan?"

"I am not sure I know what you're asking." For the first time, her voice showed something other than perfect neutrality.

Raker liked the response. Like Johnson's protest, it would draw emphasis to the answer.

"Let me see if I can help you remember," Raker said. "Have you ever been called 'Low-Ball Lannigan'?"

She shifted in her chair and blushed. "Not to my face."

"But you have heard the nickname," Raker said.

"People say all kind of things that aren't true, Mr. Raker. I heard they called you the 'Santa lawyer.' Does that mean you believe in Santa Claus?" Lannigan asked.

"Ms. Lannigan, I know why people gave me my nickname, and I'm fine with it. Believing in Santa Claus, especially at this time of year, seems like a pretty smart thing to do." With a sideways glance, he saw that a few jurors smiled. "Why do you suppose they gave you your nickname?"

"I don't know."

"Do you think it had anything to do with the hundreds of low-ball appraisals you have prepared for local governments condemning private property?"

Lannigan denied it, but Raker didn't care. Raker had planted a seed of doubt in the minds of the jurors.

Judge Stark looked at the clock and then at Raker. "Do you have much more with this witness, or should we go ahead and take our afternoon break?"

As Raker stood to answer, Twirly tugged on his coat sleeve. Raker leaned over and Twirly whispered in his ear. Standing again, he said, "Your honor, we have just a few more questions, but they won't take long."

Raker then sat down and looked at a copy of the appraisal Twirly held in his hands. It was open to Page 35. Twirly pointed at the page, and Raker looked but he didn't see anything important. Twirly whispered in his ear again. "Just zoom in on the picture and ask her about the date of the picture and what she sees in the picture. Trust me."

"I have two final questions, Ms. Lannigan."

Raker asked her to look at Page 35 of her appraisal report. It was a photo of the entire 90 acres. To make it easy for her, Johnson's associate put the page with the photo up on the courtroom monitors, including the screens in front of the jury and the witness. Raker walked to the computer providing the feed of the image and asked to use it. He then placed his finger on the keyboard and tapped to zoom in on the photograph. Everyone watched as the image of a grainy dot in the distance got closer and closer. Soon the dot began to take the shape of a structure with a fence around it. But there was something next to the structure inside the fenced area that was not yet clearly visible. When the date on the photograph became legible, Raker asked the first of his last two questions.

"Ms. Lannigan, what is the date on this photograph?"

"December 24th of last year. This was a satellite image I collected from the federal government's public database. The purpose was to show the entire property. You have focused on the stable I mentioned."

Raker continued to zoom in until the dots near the stable became clearer. The jurors leaned in toward the big monitor in front of the jury box. Then Raker asked his final question. "Ms. Lannigan, can you identify for the jury what is standing in the fenced area next to the stable?"

Lannigan put on her reading glasses and looked closely at the monitor in front of her. She took her glasses off, rubbed her eyes, placed her glasses back on and looked again. "They look like reindeer," Lannigan said. There was a murmur of interest in the audience.

"You have good eyes, Ms. Lannigan." Raker walked back to his seat next to Twirly and sat down. The jurors were still looking at the monitor.

December 22nd

3:30 p.m.

The afternoon break was only 15 minutes.

"I'll meet you in the conference room," Raker said to Twirly. He could see that Sarah lagged behind the rest of her team, so he waited to let her pass.

"Good work, Thad." Sarah put her hand on his arm but didn't linger.

He appreciated the support, even though it was brief. Being a solo practitioner was often an isolated business. A kind word from Sarah had a way of making him feel less lonely.

Austin Land approached Raker as the courtroom emptied. "I have three documents for you." Land handed them to Raker.

"Is one of them the agreement with the county?"

"It is," Land said. "My source at the government building came in handy. But there's more. I did some digging through the campaign finance records of Big Slim Thompson, and I followed the money. You may be surprised where the money trail started for one contribution. I have included a one page summary with the relevant paperwork attached."

"And the third document?" Raker asked.

"Did Twirly Masters say anything to you about something called the Vesta project?"

"No." It appeared that Twirly was still keeping secrets.

"Well, you will find this third document interesting. It is a report analyzing the defects in small machines that transport packages by air. On Page 12, there is a history of the program, and your former client, Gloria Patten, is mentioned. It seems the press was wrong about your defense of her after all."

"This is great stuff, but where did you get it?" Raker asked.

"That's the strange thing. It showed up in the mail today. The return address on the envelope simply said, North Pole."

"What do you mean, North Pole?" Raker said.

"Hey, I just report the facts," Land said.

Raker had the feeling he was getting help from several old friends. "Thanks, Austin."

"Oh, it's not free. Don't forget our deal, the exclusive." He headed for the hallway. Raker followed.

Laura, Liz and Holly waited for him outside the courtroom. Liz hugged him. "Daddy, that was great. We're pulling for you."

"We are, Mr. Raker. That was awesome about the reindeer," Holly said.

"I have to agree," Laura said. "You had me believing."

Henry Edmonds walked up. "You're doing very well, Thad. I think things will work out." Then he was gone.

Raker smiled. "Thank you all for being here. Please excuse me. I have to speak with Twirly." It was great to get compliments from his fan club, but what he really needed was for Judge Stark to round the corner, give him a high-five and tell him Twirly can keep the property.

"Raker." It was Cleve R. Johnson.

"What do you want?"

"The county is willing to up its offer from the one Sarah gave you. I'm against it, of course, because you have about as much chance of winning as I do squeezing down a chimney. But hey, it's their money. Six times tax value. That's $600,000. Your client is crazy not to take it. Matter of fact, I think he is crazy."

"Cleve, I don't care what you think about my client. Your offer is rejected. See you back in court." By the time Raker made it to the conference room, he had only a few minutes left and Twirly used up most of that time expressing his gratitude in the most loquacious way possible.

"We haven't won anything yet," Raker said.

Twirly was unconvinced. "You don't realize what you're doing, do you? With every step you take in this case, you are getting one step closer to believing again. Don't you feel it?"

"This case isn't about what I believe, Twirly."

"I think it is, Thad. You're at your best when you believe."

Raker had been frustrated with clients before, but seldom when so much was on the line. Now all he could do was usher Twirly back into the courtroom.

December 22ⁿᵈ

3:45 p.m.

Johnson called Jim Thompson, the chairman of the county commission, as his next witness. Thompson earned every bit of his nickname, Big Slim. If a person needed someone to assist in changing an overhead light bulb without a ladder, Big Slim was the man. Or maybe it was because of his gregarious personality. Back-slapping was as natural to Big Slim as saying a nonecumenical prayer before every county commission meeting.

"Tell us why you're here, Mr. Thompson," Johnson began.

"I'm here to clear things up." Big Slim smiled at the jury.

"Of course, you are," Johnson said. "Please be so kind as to do so."

"Glad to," Big Slim said. "You see, I decided we need a park, but not just something average. I wanted something that would make a difference. Something big. I put Clyde Driscole, the county manager, on the case. I said, 'Clyde, we need to do something really big to improve recreational opportunities for the residents of this fine county.' He did his part, and here we are."

"So it was your idea? That was very progressive of you. We certainly appreciate your service, Mr. Thompson."

"Call me Big Slim. Everyone does." Big Slim laughed. Johnson joined in. Raker watched the jurors' heads nodding in response. Most of them smiled.

"Big Slim, I'm sorry, but I have to ask this question. The other side in this case is claiming the county cut corners to make this happen." Johnson said this in a way that sounded like it was just pitiful that people would make such accusations. "Is that true?"

Big Slim answered in a tone that said he too was disappointed. "Mr. Johnson, I've been in politics a long time. For 20 years, I've served as an elected commissioner. And during that time, I've learned that no matter how hard public servants work, how much good we do, how much time we put into it, there are going to be people who find fault. If we provide clean water to a segment of the population, someone criticizes us for where we laid the pipes. If we build a sidewalk near a school to protect the children, someone complains about how much it costs. It's unfortunate, but it's just the way it is. You can't please everyone. That's what happened here."

"But the other side says you moved too quickly, that you didn't do an appraisal first, that the idea and location of this park were not in the county's master plan, and that the commission voted to proceed without even talking to Mr. Masters. Is all that true?" Johnson asked.

"Absolutely," Big Slim said, "and I'm not ashamed of what we did. We will pay Mr. Masters what his property is worth. And it's a great location for a park. Win-win. As chairman, I encouraged my fellow commissioners not to delay. When everyone saw what we could do for the community, the decision became a no-brainer. That's why the vote was 6-0."

Johnson thanked Big Slim and sat down. He looked thoroughly satisfied with himself.

Raker took a deep breath. "Good afternoon, sir."

"Afternoon, Mr. Raker."

"When did you first learn about my client's property?"

"As I recall, it was the day we voted to buy it."

"You mean take it, don't you?"

"One and the same!"

"Wait a minute." Raker scratched his head, like he couldn't comprehend what he was hearing. "In your 20 years of service on the county commission, you never recommended buying land for a park, and in less than one day, you become a convert, ready to jump at the chance to use government money for a park?"

"I don't care for your tone, Mr. Raker."

"I apologize, Mr. Thompson, if the question bothers you. Let me ask it a different way." Raker paused. "Before the vote occurred, there was no reference to this park in the master plan, money had not been allocated to acquire the land, and in less than one day, you went from learning about the property to orchestrating a 6-0 vote. Is that correct?"

"I didn't orchestrate anything Mr. Raker."

"But why were you in such a hurry? The county has policies and procedures for taking property from its residents and you ignored all of them. Why?"

In a tone that said he didn't much care for Raker's criticism, Big Slim replied, "I believe I explained all that."

"Right," Raker said, as if he suddenly remembered. "You suggested it was a win-win. But," Raker paused for effect, "did you tell the jury everything you learned about the property on the day of that meeting?"

He looked at the jury. They were interested now. Big Slim looked over at Johnson, who stood up in defense of Big Slim. "We object, your honor, attorney-client privilege."

"All right, ladies and gentlemen of the jury," Judge Stark said. "I need to let the lawyers talk with me without trying to impress you, so if you'll step out for a few minutes, we will take care of Mr. Johnson's objection."

When the jury was out, Judge Stark said to Johnson, "Would you care to explain how the answer to Mr. Raker's question is privileged?"

"I met with Mr. Thompson before the county commission meeting that day and gave him advice about the property," Johnson said. "What we discussed is privileged."

Big Slim concurred. "That's right. I was getting advice from our lawyer, Mr. Johnson."

Raker knew this objection was a ploy to divert attention from the agreement, which he had in his possession, thanks to Austin Land. "Your honor," he said, "I don't intend to ask Mr. Thompson about the advice he received from the county's attorney."

"Bring them back," Judge Stark told the bailiff. When the jurors were settled, he told Raker to proceed but to rephrase his last question.

"Mr. Thompson," Raker said, "Did you learn about and sign a written agreement related to the property on the day of the county commission meeting?"

"Maybe," Big Slim said.

"Let me refresh your recollection." Raker approached the witness with the document, and handed a copy to Johnson on the way. He handed another copy to Judge Stark. Before Raker was able to ask his next question, Johnson interrupted.

"May we approach, your honor?"

Judge Stark waved them up and covered the microphone on the bench with his right hand. Some of the jurors leaned in, no doubt hoping to hear something interesting.

"Judge," Johnson whispered, "the prejudicial effect of this document outweighs any possible relevance for what the jury needs to decide."

Judge Stark flipped through the document. He then said to Johnson in a low voice: "I assume your point is that this document does not relate to the issue of the fair market value of the property."

Johnson nodded. "Exactly."

Judge Stark waved the attorneys back to their tables. He then said, "For the time being, the objection is sustained. Mr. Raker, until I hear more, you cannot ask about this document. Do you have any other questions?"

Raker was discouraged. The document was his big surprise. He hoped to use it to show the jury how the county was conspiring with Hank Snow to use the land for more than a park. The consolation was that Judge Stark now knew the truth.

"No further questions," Raker said.

"Mr. Johnson, anything else?"

Johnson looked confident. "The county rests its case."

Judge Stark turned in his chair. "Bailiff, sign us out until 9:30 tomorrow morning."

December 23rd

9:30 a.m.

"Call your first witness, Mr. Raker," Judge Stark said.

"We call Twirly Masters."

Raker's plan was not to ask Masters questions about his real work at the Haints. He was sure Johnson wouldn't be able to resist those questions himself, and he wanted what Masters said about that to come out on cross-examination. It would look less rehearsed and more believable. Plus, Johnson might end up looking like a bully. His advice to his client had been, whatever Johnson asks you, tell the truth.

After Masters was sworn in, Raker asked him to state his name for the record. "Twirly Masters," he said. "I'm told it's a family name. I can't be sure, but that seems logical. My daddy's name was Masters, as was his daddy before him. No one knows where the name Twirly came from. But I have a hunch. Perhaps —"

"Mr. Masters," Judge Stark interrupted. "We'd like to finish in time for Christmas, so here's what I need you to do. When your lawyer asks you a question, try to answer that question. Mr. Raker asked you to state your name. I'm pretty sure you dealt with that question in the first two words you spoke. That would have been the time to stop."

"I'm sorry, Mr. Judge, sir. I have a habit of being a little long-winded sometimes. I will do my best."

"See that you do, Mr. Masters." Judge Stark motioned for Raker to continue.

"Mr. Masters," Raker said, "please tell the jury how long the property has been in your family."

"A long, long time. Too long, to be exact. My great-great-great-grandparents were the first to lease the property and those lease rights got passed down and extended during each generation. A wonderful family venture."

"What do you mean by lease rights?" Raker asked.

"My family had the right to live on the property for many generations. In exchange, we provided an important service to our landlord. It's been a splendid place to live and work."

"Do you own the property now?"

"Yes, sir," Masters said. "I have a copy of the deed on display at the house. Makes for a real conversation piece as to how I got it. Yes, it does. Would you like me to tell the story?"

Sensing Judge Stark's impatience from the corner of his eye, Raker said, "That won't be necessary, but thank you. Can you tell us about the property?"

"Yes. As everyone knows, I live on 90 acres. It's beautiful land. My house is on the tallest point about half a mile from the highway. From the front stoop, I can see most of the county. From the back of the house, I have a wonderful view of the rolling landscape below. Just spectacular. Breeze is nice up there too. One time — "

"Mr. Masters," Judge Stark admonished, "I think you've answered the question."

"How long have you lived there?" Raker asked.

"Most of my life. I hope to be buried there one day, assuming I don't get kicked off the property first."

"Do you know the property pretty well, Mr. Masters?"

"Like the nose on my face. I can't miss it, even when I'm not looking in the mirror. At my nose, that is. But, yes, I know the property very well."

"Can you tell the jury, based on your experience with the property, your opinion of the fair market value of the property?" Raker was taking a gamble. He wanted Masters to offer an opinion on value because it might be higher than what an expert he could hire might offer.

"Mr. Masters?"

Twirly started to say something and then smiled. "I can't do it," Masters said.

"And why is that? Why can't you do it?"

Twirly Masters turned toward the jury, and for once, he was serious. "I can only tell you what it is worth to me." Twirly's answer was logical but it wasn't helping to establish an objectively reasonable value of his property. At least the jury might see him as an honest witness.

Twirly smiled his optimistic smile. "The county doesn't have enough money to pay me what the property is worth. Not today. Not tomorrow. Not next month. Not next year. Sure, the property is a great place to live and work, but it's much more. It's a place that brings genuine surprise and happiness to those who believe, every single Christmas. You can't replace something that valuable with money. No, siree. There are some things in life that are worth more than the end of a rainbow's pot of gold."

Raker was satisfied that he'd done his best with Twirly Masters so he turned him over to Johnson.

"Mr. Masters," Johnson began. "I'm curious about your testimony that your property is a great place to work. Are you running a business on your property?"

"You might say that," Masters said. "It's a nonprofit operation."

"And what is the name of the company you work for?"

"North Pole Enterprises," Masters said. He didn't flinch.

"Wait," Johnson said. "The same company Hank Snow works for?"

"One and the same," Masters said.

"But I thought North Pole Enterprises was your landlord until recently."

"It was," Masters said. "As I explained, I provide a service to my landlord."

"What do you do?" Johnson asked.

Masters looked at Raker, who nodded his approval. Full steam ahead was the message. Raker knew it wouldn't be long before Twirly's enthusiasm for Christmas filled the courtroom.

"I work in distribution." Twirly said.

Johnson pressed. "This wouldn't be distribution for some magical purpose, would it?"

"It's not magical to me. It's a way of life."

"I will cut to the chase, Mr. Masters. Do you think you work for Santa Claus?"

Twirly paused before he answered. The courtroom was quiet, because everyone wanted to know the answer. Then Twirly asked Johnson a question. "Did you know, Mr. Johnson, that distribution is the key to any good business?"

"Excuse me?"

"Without good distribution, presents don't arrive on time, or at all. They just don't. Hard as you might try, they don't. It takes planning and execution and a lot of coordination."

"Hold on. Are you talking about distribution of Christmas presents?"

"Yes, indeed, Mr. Johnson. Yes, indeed," Twirly said.

"So you admit it. You believe you work for Santa Claus."

"No, Mr. Johnson." Twirly smiled. "I know I work for Santa Claus. He's my boss. He's also president of North Pole Enterprises, which until recently was my landlord. Three days ago, he deeded the property to me. He and I go way back."

Johnson and everyone on the county's side of the courtroom, other than Sarah Kennedy, started to laugh, but not for long.

"Order," Judge Stark said. He banged his gavel hard.

"Excuse me, your honor," Johnson said, wiping tears of laughter from his eyes. "I hadn't really expected Mr. Masters to admit to such a thing."

Raker noticed that some of the jurors were looking at Masters in a new light. Some appeared surprised. Others seemed sympathetic.

"Do you have any more questions for the witness?" Judge Stark asked.

"I do," Johnson said.

"Mr. Masters, I understand distribution is important, but if it is true what you say about your boss, don't you have a sleigh and flying reindeer for that?"

"Are you mocking me, Mr. Johnson? Sounds like it, by the tone of your voice. But it's a good question, so I'm just checking. Just want to be sure you're serious before I answer. Want to get this right. Yes, I do."

"Not at all, Mr. Masters. I'm not mocking you. I am just trying to understand the facts."

"Well then, let me explain. We do rely on magic for deliveries, but like the gasoline for your car, it only goes so far."

"I don't understand." Johnson made a big gesture with his hands trying to draw the jury into his feigned puzzlement.

"In recent years, we've been using more and more magic to meet an increased demand for production of presents caused by an expanding world population. I was told that, in order to compensate for this, the plan is to use less magic when we deliver the presents, by using drones instead."

"And who told you this?" Johnson asked.

"Hank Snow."

"Did you say Hank Snow," Johnson asked, "the chief operating officer of North Pole Enterprises?"

"That's his title," Twirly said, "but I don't answer to him. No, sir, not at all. As for the company and what it really does, he knows the truth."

"Well, what is the truth?" Johnson asked, his voice rising in anticipation.

"It's international, all right, but it's not the way he makes it sound. But hey, he's right there," Twirly said, pointing at Hank Snow, who sat on the county's side of the courtroom. "Ask him about it. And while you're at it, why don't you ask him why he's helping you, Mr. Johnson? Ask him why an international toy company, if that's what he claims to work for, is trying to put a distribution division of his own company out of business. Maybe he will tell the truth, but I doubt it. I surely do."

"I don't have to ask him, Mr. Masters. I can ask you," Johnson said. "Why do you think Mr. Snow wants to put you out of business?"

"Hank Snow is drawn to technology like a piece of metal to a magnet. He's like a kitty cat obsessed with a ball of twine. He's always scratching at it, looking for a new way of doing things. Yes, he is."

"What's wrong with that?" Johnson asked.

"Simple. His motives are not in line with Santa's mission," Twirly said.

Johnson looked at Judge Stark as if he couldn't believe what he was hearing. Judge Stark looked back at Johnson as if he knew something Johnson didn't. Raker glanced at the jury. Their faces displayed a mixture of curiosity and surprise.

"With Hank Snow," Twirly said, "if technology puts people out of work, it's just another day at the office. Just another day. If the technology is defective, it doesn't matter. Not at all. If the technology is dangerous, it's an acceptable risk. Just always. The problem with Hank Snow is that he has the mind of a dog chasing a fast car. He always thinks he can catch it. Yes, he does. And goodness, gracious, when it comes to technology, we dare not put him in the driver's seat. He will outrun his headlights every day. And I mean, for sure."

"And is that where the drones come in?" Johnson was sarcastic.

"Yes, it is. But you need some background first. Always start at the beginning, my lawyer says." Twirly looked at the jury. "The worldwide Christmas grid is divided into zones and the zones are divided into districts. My property serves as the distribution center for Zone 24, which covers 30 Christmas districts, including the district that takes in this county." Twirly paused.

"Please go on, Mr. Masters."

It was clear to Raker that Johnson thought the more Twirly talked, the less believable he became. Raker was beginning to smile now, because if anyone could talk his way out of a hole, it was Twirly Masters.

"The distribution centers serve two purposes. First, we're like the Pony Express stations in the Old

West where riders would stop to rest their mounts. The stable your appraiser talked about is used for that purpose. We call it the reindeer paddock. Reindeer can fly but they need to rest and eat along the way. Flying around the world uses up some serious calories. Yes, it does."

The courtroom hadn't been this quiet in days. The silence made Raker nervous but hopeful.

Twirly continued. "When Santa and his sleigh come into our zone, we restock the sleigh."

"Hold on," Johnson said, "I thought the presents were made at the North Pole."

"So you do believe, Mr. Johnson."

A few jurors smiled.

"Not at all, Mr. Masters. If this weren't such a waste of time, it would be comical."

Twirly shrugged his shoulders. "Most of the presents are made at the North Pole and shipped to us by rail in December so we can organize and code them for delivery. But many children wait until the last week to make up their minds, or they change their minds at the last minute. Can't blame them, really. Just too many commercials on TV. Yes, too many. That's why we have a production team at the Haints, so we can fill those last-minute requests. You of all people should know about that, Mr. Johnson."

"What are you talking about?" Johnson sounded genuinely puzzled.

"Just last year, your son asked for a football jersey on Christmas Eve after the stores were closed. Very popular item, very popular indeed. Even if the stores had been open, you couldn't have found it. The jersey had been sold out for weeks."

"How could you possibly know that?"

"We have collectors who monitor the behavior and requests of the children. Henry Edmonds is a collector and a good friend of mine, fabulous at his job. He alerted me to your son's request and we were able to fill it with one of our tailors at the Haints. He did get the jersey, didn't he?"

"Yes, but my wife —"

"You cross-examined her like you've been coming after me. She chose the easy way and just said she bought it. I admired her for it, yes I did. She took the direct approach, and you were none the wiser. Maybe I should have done that today. Yes, indeed."

Johnson's confident demeanor had slipped a notch.

"Would you like me to finish, Mr. Johnson?"

Johnson said nothing. Judge Stark leaned toward the microphone. "Proceed, Mr. Masters. The jury and I would like to hear the rest."

Twirly continued. "Seven years ago, Hank Snow had the idea of using drones to replace the way Santa Claus delivers Christmas presents. Can you imagine? I know, hard to believe. Out with what works, in with the uncertain. Anyway, rather than Santa and his sleigh, Snow wanted to fill the sky with little red flying machines. Snow even had a name for the contraption. He called it the Vesta, named after the Roman goddess of hearth, home and family. I know, I looked it up on the Internet. Anyway, he ran a series of secret field tests in this district to prove the Vesta's worth, but there were problems with the tests. Here's the worst part. Yes, the very worst. At the time, he didn't tell anyone at the North Pole that he knew about a design flaw. That flaw lead to Ms. Patten's accident and the trial lost by Mr. Raker. Very sad time, very sad, indeed."

"What does the Patten trial have to do with the use of drones to deliver Christmas presents?" Johnson seemed surprised by his own question, as if his curiosity had overruled his plotting.

"Ms. Patten drove her car off Highway 11 near my property and killed Mr. Ledbetter's three best cows: Mable, Bessie and Gertrude. The rest of the cattle stampeded the property, damaging the fencing, farm equipment and winter crop. She told the court that little red flying machines dropped presents from the sky on Christmas Eve, causing her to run off the road. It sounded far-fetched and the jury didn't believe her. But her story was true."

"Is that so?" Johnson asked.

"Absolutely. On the night of the accident, we hustled out there, yes, we did, and we picked up those presents, rewrapped them and delivered them on time. While we were there, we bagged and removed all the parts and pieces from the wrecked drones, and we cleaned that place from east to west and north to south. Made the ground look even better than it did before. And that's why Ms. Patten lost and why Mr. Raker took a beating in the press; there was no evidence of what caused the accident. In the end, things worked out. Yes, they did. I reached out to Ms. Patten and she came to work for me; she's worked at the Haints ever since. Oh, and Mr. Raker became the lawyer he is today."

"You have people working in that broken-down house of yours?"

"I wouldn't call it broken-down. You can't judge a book by its cover, you know. But yes, I have people working there. Of all ages."

"What's the average age of the people who work for you?"

Masters looked like he was doing a calculation in his head, and then he started counting on his fingers. "Probably, average age is around 200 years. Of course, some are much older and I have one young elf-in-training. She's here in the courtroom." Masters waved to Holly.

Johnson looked troubled. Twirly smiled. "Come on, Mr. Johnson. You know what you want to ask."

"You want this jury to believe there are elves working in your home?"

"Mr. Johnson, I have to give you credit. You are getting smarter and smarter as this trial goes on."

Raker noticed that the jurors were fully attentive. They looked as if they weren't going to miss anything Twirly had to say.

Then, Johnson asked one question too many. "So why do you think Mr. Snow is trying to push you off the property?"

"Two reasons. One, Hank Snow never forgave me for reporting to Santa Claus that the Vesta program ran a nice woman off the road and sent three cows to heaven. That's a definite truth. And two, he wants to use my property as a base for drone deliveries. But you knew that already."

"I knew no such thing," Johnson said.

"Of course, you did —"

"Wait, Mr. Masters, I didn't ask you a question —"

"You drafted the agreement between Hank Snow and the county," Twirly said. "Yes, you did."

"Objection. Move to strike!" Johnson shouted. "Your honor, that testimony is not admissible."

"Seems to me, Mr. Johnson, that you opened the door to that one," Judge Stark said. "Your objection is overruled."

"Never mind then," Johnson said. "That's all the questions I have for this witness."

Raker saw Johnson stagger a bit as he returned to his chair.

"No redirect, your honor, and no further witnesses," Raker said. He was counting on Johnson to make another mistake by putting Hank Snow on the stand.

"Mr. Johnson, would you like to call any rebuttal witnesses?" Judge Stark asked.

Johnson took a moment to huddle with his team. He came out of the scrum and said, "The county will call Mr. Hank Snow in rebuttal."

Judge Stark looked at the clock and decided to take an early lunch. "Be back at 1:00," he said, "and we will hear what Mr. Snow has to say."

December 23ʳᵈ

1:00 p.m.

"The county calls Hank Snow," Johnson said.

"Come up and be sworn Mr. Snow," Judge Stark said. "As I recall, you've done this before." Snow walked defiantly up to the witness box, took the oath and sat down. He nodded to the jury, but he didn't look at Judge Stark.

"Mr. Snow," Johnson began. "Were you in the courtroom this morning when Twirly Masters testified?"

"I was."

"And what did you think of Mr. Masters' testimony?" Johnson asked.

"I think Mr. Masters has an interesting imagination."

"So he wasn't telling the truth about working for Santa Claus?"

"No," Snow said. "I'm surprised I even have to answer the question."

Raker knew the jurors would be interested in Mr. Snow, but suspicious, too. He couldn't match Twirly for likeability.

"He says you developed a program to use drones to replace Santa and his reindeer. Is that true?"

"Mr. Johnson, the next thing you know, Mr. Masters will have me inventing motorized skateboards to deliver Thanksgiving turkeys."

"Then who do you work for?" Johnson asked.

"As I have explained before in this very courthouse, the name of my company is North Pole Enterprises. It is an international toy company authorized to do business under the laws of the state of Delaware. We sell toys all over the world."

"But not with Santa Claus?"

"No, sir. Not with Santa Claus." Snow was emphatic.

"Mr. Snow," Johnson said, "there appears to be some confusion about the roles you and Mr. Masters play for North Pole Enterprises. Could you explain these roles?"

"Mr. Masters is responsible for a segment of our distribution business that covers about 10 states in the U.S. He has been with the company for many years. I have no problem with his work ethic. I am the chief operating officer. While he doesn't report to me directly, he does report to our senior officer in distribution, who reports to me."

"So, if you know, why does Mr. Masters hold such animosity toward you?"

"For the past 45 years, he's been left alone to do his work. He's become resistant to innovation and is opposed to the use of new technology. To stay competitive, and to keep our customers satisfied, we have to change with the times. If we don't, we will be left behind. But Mr. Masters is one of those people who refuse to accept change, and he blames me for making him face that reality. As a manager, I have seen this in a number of older employees. Eventually, they can't keep up and they don't make it. They usually retire rather than try something new. Mr. Masters just became angry instead."

Raker saw a few of the younger jurors nod, as if they understood, perhaps seeing this happen with employees in their own workplaces.

"We've heard from Mr. Masters about the drones," Johnson said. "Has that been one of the points of disagreement Mr. Masters has had with you?"

"Yes," Snow said. "For the past 10 years, I have had a small team of professionals studying ways to improve our delivery system. The use of drones is one of those options. With more presents to deliver by Christmas Day, we have to be more creative, because that day is the most important deadline for our business. The presents have to arrive on time. If they don't, we won't have much of a business."

"Mr. Masters says you have been reckless and uncaring with technology."

"As I said, he has difficulty with change."

"So you're not out to destroy Christmas?"

"Of course not. I want the same things he does. I want the company to succeed and I want the presents to get to the children on time so they will be happy."

"Then why were you unwilling to extend his lease and willing to give the property to the county?"

"We discussed this at length in my senior staff summer planning retreat. The house is in disrepair.

You heard the appraiser; it's a tear-down. And frankly, we've outgrown the space it offers. Continuing to use an old house for a 10-state distribution center didn't seem like a smart idea to senior staff so we voted to give the property to the county. Also, the stable is better suited for use by the county for a park."

"What about the reindeer that Mr. Raker so dramatically showed to the jury?"

Snow laughed. "Marketing," he said. "I thought it was a great idea. We brought in reindeer at Christmas to make the company look more connected to the holiday."

"Now that you've straightened all that out," Johnson said, "can you explain why you've been cooperating with the county on this case?"

As Snow started to answer, he looked toward the defense table where Raker and Twirly sat, made eye contact with Twirly Masters and looked away quickly.

"I'm sorry," Snow said, "could you repeat the question?"

"Of course," Johnson said. "Please explain why you have been helping the county."

"It's very simple," Snow said. "North Pole Enterprises is in business to make money, but we are not without a soul; we give back to the communities where we do business. We have a parks program that allows us to donate land when it ceases to be useful to the operation. I knew the lease on our Highway 11 property was due to expire in December and I thought it would make a nice park. After senior staff made its decision, I informed Mr. Driscole and Mr. Thompson in September that when the lease expired, my company would donate the property to the county; the only condition was that the county must use it for a park. It was our goal to make the children and their families in this community happy."

His chest inflated, Johnson turned to Raker and said, "Your witness."

Twirly patted Raker on the back to provide encouragement. Raker went to work. "Good afternoon, Mr. Snow," Raker said.

Snow nodded, but said nothing.

"It's been about 12 years since we last talked, correct?" Raker asked.

"If you say so," Snow responded.

"It was at the trial of Henry Edmonds, the man seated behind me here in the courtroom. Surely you remember that trial?" Raker asked.

"I remember. You twisted the truth when you cross-examined me, which I presume is what you are going to try to do now."

173

Raker ignored the hostility. "After the trial of Mr. Edmonds, you were promoted, correct?"

"Yes. I was promoted from head of security to chief operating officer."

"Congratulations!" Raker waited for a response but Snow said nothing.

"Mr. Snow," Raker said, "You're pretty obsessed with drones, aren't you?"

Snow looked to Johnson, who reacted quickly. "Objection," he said. "Immaterial, irrelevant and disrespectful!"

Judge Stark cleared his throat. "Mr. Johnson, you have a short memory. You just got through asking Mr. Masters questions about drones. It's Mr. Raker's turn to have his fun with your witness. Overruled."

Snow waited until prompted again by Raker. "I am familiar with drones," he said.

"Have you had any experience working with them?"

"What difference does that make?"

"A lot, but we will get to that in a moment," Raker said. "Can you explain why the property has a stable on it that is used for reindeer every Christmas Eve?"

"I just explained that the reindeer gig was a one-time publicity stunt," Snow said.

"Speaking of reindeer," Raker said, "would you say that reindeer are the most efficient way to deliver presents at Christmas?"

"No," Snow said, "it's —"

Snow caught himself, but not in time. Everyone in the courtroom saw his discomfort. He was in a spot and Cleve R. Johnson couldn't rescue him.

"Would drones be a better way to go?" Raker asked.

"Objection," Johnson said.

Raker couldn't have been more pleased with the timing of Johnson's objection, and Judge Stark was quick to emphasize the question to the jury when he responded, "Overruled."

"You call it the Vesta program, don't you?" Raker asked. Snow didn't answer. "I have the report right here. Shall I read from it?" Again, Snow was silent.

"Mr. Snow," Judge Stark said, "you need to answer the question."

Snow blurted out, "The program is experimental. And it is a trade secret. I won't talk about it further. I won't share information publicly for our competitors to exploit."

"But that program is why you're here, isn't it?" Raker asked.

"I'm here because your client is a fraud." Snow's earlier composure had disappeared.

"Is he a fraud, or is he someone who, at risk to his own livelihood, is willing to stand up to the man whose technology schemes are threatening Christmas?"

"No, he's a fraud. He wants this court to believe in fantasy. And he talks too much; he can't keep a secret. He should take the money the county is offering so the county can build the park."

"You never liked the fact that the truth about Christmas came out in the Edmonds trial, did you?" Raker asked.

"Your truth, not mine." Snow had his arms crossed and was not budging.

"Mr. Snow," Raker said, "let me ask you about a statement you made a few minutes ago. You told the jury that the only condition on your company's gift to the county was that the property be used as a park. That isn't true, is it?" He held up a document as he asked the question.

Snow looked at Raker holding the document and then at Johnson. His eyes suggested he needed help.

"Objection," Johnson said, "he's trying to introduce the document the court said was inadmissible."

Judge Stark looked at Johnson, then at Raker and then at the document Raker was holding in his hand. "Mr. Johnson, he did not ask him about the document. He asked him whether he was telling the truth in my courtroom about his statement that there was only one condition on the gift to the county. Objection overruled."

Raker held the document up a little higher and asked the question again. "Were you telling the truth, Mr. Snow, about the condition to the gift?"

Raker knew he was gambling. If Snow lied about the condition, Raker was holding the document to prove the lie, but he might not be able to use it if Judge Stark stuck to his earlier ruling. Snow took his time to answer. Raker suspected that Snow was deciding whether it was worth the risk.

"Mr. Snow," Judge Stark said, "I have seen the document Mr. Raker is holding in his hand, so think very carefully before you answer."

Another 30 seconds passed and Snow made up his mind. "No," he said.

"Does that mean you weren't telling the truth?" Raker asked.

"I didn't tell everything. It's not the same as a lie," Snow said.

"What did you leave out?"

"My company will keep some residual rights to the property. That's all. It's nothing important."

"Did your company retain the right to use the air space over the property?" Raker asked.

"Possibly," Snow said.

"And did your company retain the right to use the storage building?"

"Yes, it will be a perfect place for us to keep inventory. We are in the business of selling toys, remember." Snow was petulant.

"Why is construction work planned for the building?"

"Repair work to the roof," Snow replied.

"Ah, yes, the roof," Raker said. "After Ms. Lannigan, the county's appraiser, said the storage building had no value because it needed a new roof, I decided to take a look for myself after court that day. When I did, I ran into a man at the building who will be supervising your work. He was kind enough to show me the plans. From what I observed, you are planning more than repairs. You're going to build a retractable roof over the entire storage area, aren't you?"

"I don't have to explain my company's plans to you. It's a private business," Snow said.

"I agree, your honor," Johnson said. "This line of questioning is improper. North Pole Enterprises is not on trial here. We object."

"It goes to the real purpose of the taking, your honor," Raker said. "Mr. Snow says he works for a private company. Therefore, this evidence supports the fact that the county is taking my client's property for a private purpose."

"But that is for the court to decide," Johnson said. "It's irrelevant to the value of the property."

Raker didn't let up. "This evidence is also for impeachment. Mr. Snow is a key witness for the county. Truth matters."

"I agree," Judge Stark said. "The objection is overruled."

"Mr. Snow," Raker continued, "isn't it true that the roof you plan to build will retract to open a storage area the length and width of a football field?"

"That's about the size of it," Snow snapped.

"Mr. Snow, isn't it also true that you've harbored a grudge against Mr. Masters for some time?" Raker asked.

"Not true."

"Isn't it also true that you hatched a plan to remove Mr. Masters from the property because you didn't have the power to fire him without approval from the president?"

"Not true."

"Isn't it also true that the plan to remove Mr. Masters from the property involved help from the county?" Raker was holding the same document up in his hand again.

"Not true."

Raker changed direction. "You gave Big Slim Thompson a real incentive, didn't you?"

"I don't follow your question."

"Did you hear Big Slim testify on Tuesday?"

"Yes," Snow replied.

"He said the taking of the property was a no-brainer."

"It was," Snow said.

"But why was that necessary if the property was a gift?"

"I knew Twirly Masters would make up a story about a lease extension. I was right."

"But you didn't know that the president of your company would sign a deed to convey the property to Mr. Masters, did you?"

"No." Snow hung his head.

"The president is your boss, right?"

"He is," Snow said.

"Why would the president deed the property to Mr. Masters two days ago if he had wanted to give the property to the county?"

"I really don't know."

"Is the president loyal to his employees?" Raker asked.

"He is," Snow said.

"And do you trust him to do the right thing?" Raker put Snow on the spot.

Snow frowned. "I trust him."

"To do the right thing?" Raker pressed. He wasn't letting Snow off the hook.

"Sure," Snow said, but the way he squirmed suggested the opposite.

"How long have you known him?" Raker asked.

"Hundreds of —"

"Go on," Raker said, "were you about to say hundreds of years?"

"I misspoke." The bravado that carried Snow to the witness stand was almost gone.

"About that no-brainer," Raker said. "What was the incentive for Big Slim Thompson?"

"To provide a park for the community," Snow said. "He is a good public servant."

"I mean the financial incentive," Raker said.

Snow looked at Johnson and Johnson turned to look at Thompson, who tugged at his necktie. Johnson stood quickly. "Your honor, I fail to see how this question has any bearing on the fair market value of the property. We object."

"The objection is overruled." Judge Stark's voice resounded through the courtroom.

"Mr. Snow," Raker said, "I'm talking about the campaign contribution from North Pole Enterprises to Big Slim's election campaign."

"Mr. Raker, I realize you look for conspiracies in all your cases, but giving money to politicians is not a crime. Our company needs to work with government officials and Mr. Thompson has done a lot of volunteer work for the community. We thought it appropriate to support his campaign."

"Does that explain why you went to great lengths to hide it, by running the contribution through a recently created shell corporation?"

"Mr. Raker, I don't write the checks. You will have to ask someone in our accounting department why it was handled that way."

"Let me see if I have this right, Mr. Snow." Raker acted puzzled. "First, you claim there is no connection between your company and Santa Claus. Second, you dispute that Ms. Patten was attacked by little red drones of your making. Third, you testify that the only condition on the gift of the land is that it be used as a park, and then you admit to an agreement with the county to retain air rights and storage space on the property. Finally, you don't know why Big Slim's big check from your company went through a recently created shell corporation. Did I get all that right?"

"Where are you going with this, Mr. Raker?" Snow asked.

"A better question," Raker said, "is where you are going with little red drones that will be stored in a building the size of a football field and then launched through a retractable roof into the air space above? Is that another trade secret? Or are we getting closer and closer to the truth?"

Snow didn't answer, but Raker had a lawyer's intuition that his words had sunk in with everyone in the courtroom.

"A few final questions," Raker said. "Isn't it true that when you approached the county in September, you had a well-conceived plan? You were going to offer the property to the county so that you could displace the old ways of distributing Christmas presents with a new drone program?"

Snow didn't answer, and Raker continued. "The county would get the property for a park, Twirly Masters and his workers would have to leave said property and you would get to distribute presents with flying machines, correct?"

Again, there was no response by Snow.

"But you had to modify your plan when Twirly Masters decided to put up a legal fight, didn't you? So you destroyed the lease extension. But that didn't work either, because your boss, the president of North Pole Enterprises, felt such loyalty to Mr. Masters that he deeded the property to him a few days ago, didn't he?"

Snow just sat there, fuming.

"And that is when you took the risk of testifying, hoping to conceal the true nature of your deal with the county. Does that about cover it, Mr. Snow?"

"Objection," Johnson said. "Compound question." But there was little conviction in his tone.

Raker looked at the jury and then at Judge Stark. "I am confident that the jury now knows the answers to these questions, so I will withdraw them." Raker sat down. For the second time in 12 years, he was done with Hank Snow.

December 23rd

2:30 p.m.

Judge Stark sent the jury home until the next morning and told the lawyers it was time for him to rule on whether the county had the right to take the property. He was ready to hear final arguments on the issue.

Raker went first, arguing that the county had acted arbitrarily and capriciously by not following its normal procedures for condemning property. More importantly, the county had entered into a secret agreement with Hank Snow. Plus, there was a problem with the drones.

"And what are they going to be used for, Mr. Raker?" Judge Stark asked.

Raker knew that Judge Stark was teasing him. "Your honor, the testimony offered by Mr. Snow and Mr. Masters is conflicting on that point, but it doesn't really matter. The use of drones could be dangerous, not to mention ineffective."

"You mean children might not get their gifts on Christmas morning from Santa Claus if something goes wrong?"

Raker felt he wasn't going to win over Judge Stark with this line of argument. Instead, he decided to capitalize on Snow's testimony that North Pole Enterprises is a private company.

"The county," he said, "is simply doing Mr. Snow's dirty work of acquiring the property for use by Snow's private business. That makes the intended purpose of the taking perfectly clear. It is for a private, not a public, purpose."

When it was Johnson's turn, he did the smart thing, in Raker's opinion. He had Sarah make the legal argument for the county. When she stood up, she gave Raker a sympathetic look. She then received permission from Judge Stark to approach the bench where she handed him copies of two appellate court opinions. Those precedents, she argued, do not require that a taking of private property be entirely for a public purpose, provided the main purpose of the taking is for the public. The evidence is clear, Sarah argued, that the property will be used for a park. Any incidental use for Mr. Snow's company does not destroy the main purpose and validity of the taking.

After the arguments, Judge Stark read the case law Kennedy had given him and looked over his notes. The parties and their lawyers waited. The audience was quiet, but there was tension in the air on Raker's side of the courtroom. He glanced over his shoulder. Liz and Holly were holding hands. Henry had his arm around Liz. Laura had her hands clasped together on her knees. Austin Land had stopped typing on his computer.

"Mr. Raker," Judge Stark said, "At the initial hearing in this case, I didn't think you had much of a chance. But you brought out interesting evidence. The county manager and the chairman of the county commission cut corners and made deals they kept secret from the public. Without this trial, the information would not have come out. I commend you for your tenacity.

"Ms. Kennedy," he continued, "you presented very persuasive case law, and your arguments are sound. You have done a good job making the case for the county." He paused, looking a bit uncomfortable with what he had to do. Raker took a deep breath.

"The ruling of the court," Judge Stark said, "is that the condemnation of the property is legal; the taking is for a valid public purpose."

Raker exhaled. It was over. They had lost.

"Mr. Johnson," Judge Stark continued, "by my estimate, we should finish the trial and have a jury verdict by midday on Christmas Eve. Will the county be able to deposit the amount of the verdict with the clerk of court at that time?"

Johnson looked at Clyde Driscole who nodded in the affirmative. "Yes, your honor, the funds will be ready," Johnson said.

"Mr. Raker," Judge Stark said. "I hate to be the bearer of bad news, but when the verdict comes in and the county makes the deposit, your client will need to vacate the property immediately. I know it's Christmas Eve, but I can't help the timing. He should make preparations tonight."

Judge Stark looked from Raker to Johnson. "Closing arguments to the jury will begin in the morning. It should be a wonderful way for us to spend Christmas Eve." He banged his gavel hard on the bench and exited the courtroom.

Reality was setting in. Raker thought of everyone who had depended upon him to pull off a Christmas miracle, but it wouldn't happen. When he turned to look at Liz, he saw that her eyes had clouded up. Holly hung her head. Land looked troubled as he typed away on his laptop. Edmonds kept the same calm demeanor he had always exhibited in court. Only Masters remained upbeat. He put his arm around Raker and said in a confident voice: "Never give up hope, Thad. Always believe!"

Henry Edmonds was watching the celebration that was taking place on the other side of the courtroom. He saw Johnson's entire legal team, except Sarah Kennedy, congratulate Johnson as if it were he, not Kennedy, who was responsible for the victory. He saw her pack her laptop and walk down the aisle. He knew what he had to do. He whispered encouragement to Liz and Holly and then followed her into the hallway. When he caught up to her, he touched her lightly on the shoulder.

"Excuse me, Ms. Kennedy," he said. "May I have a word?"

She looked wary, as he suspected she would. "I'd better not speak with you, Mr. Edmonds. I still represent the county, and whatever you tell me, I may have to use against Mr. Masters."

"Don't worry," Edmonds said. "It's not about Twirly. It's about Thad."

"What about Thad?"

"I think he's in love with you."

"You've misunderstood," Kennedy said. "Until today, we were good friends, but after what just happened, I doubt he will ever want to speak with me again. It's time for me to move away from this county. This trial has made me feel like I'm on the opposite side of what's right. I need a fresh start."

"I think you underestimate Thad Raker, Ms. Kennedy. What's the expression? Yes, I have it. He keeps his feelings close to his vest. I've been watching him watching you. He respects you a great deal. And another thing . . ." Edmonds paused.

"Yes," Sarah said. "What is it?"

"It's never too late," Henry said.

"Never too late for what?" Kennedy asked.

Edmonds patted her on the shoulder, wished her a Merry Christmas and walked away. In his pocket was Liz Raker's letter to Santa Claus. She wanted just one thing for Christmas and Edmonds had been designated by Santa Claus to make it happen.

December 23rd

8:45 p.m.

"I have an idea," Liz said. She and Holly had been scheming about how they might help her dad and Twirly since the judge made his decision that the county could take the property. They were spending the night at her Aunt Laura's house, in order to give Raker and Twirly the chance to prepare for closing arguments. They were in their pajamas on the double bed they were sharing in the guest room.

"I'm all ears," Holly joked, pointing at her left ear.

"You know," Liz said, "now that you mention it, it is getting a little more pointed."

Holly smiled.

"So I've been thinking about The Archives you mentioned," Liz said. "Is there any way we can look at it?"

"I don't have access to it, but I know someone who does. What's your plan?"

Liz told her what she had in mind, and Holly said, "I like it."

Holly took out her cellphone and pressed an odd-looking key featuring the letters "AB."

"Is that some kind of hotline button?" Liz asked.

"It's how I get in touch with my mentor. AB. Always Believe," Holly said.

A minute later Liz felt the presence of another person in the room. She turned her head to see a person sitting on the dresser, legs crossed, looking at Liz and Holly with a smile on her face. Her long blond hair flowed wispily over ears that were pointed at the tops. She wore green tights, curved-toe shoes, a lacy top and a felt hat.

"A very good evening to the both of you," she said.

"Liz," Holly said, "this is Snowflake. She's an elf from the North Pole."

Liz looked closely at Snowflake and it was true, she looked every bit like an elf. She had the hat, the shoes, the ears and, more importantly, she had appeared out of nowhere. She wondered if this was truth hitting her in the face, just like her dad said might happen.

"How is your dear wise father?" Snowflake asked.

"You know my dad?"

"We worked on a case together 12 years ago," Snowflake said. "Your father kept a good man from going to jail, and he saved Christmas. He is a very smart person."

"So the story is true?" Liz asked.

"As true as Christmas! Your father is a legal legend where I come from."

"I wish he felt that way. He's been so down on himself. And he's lonely. I worry what will happen if he loses this case."

"But you have an idea?" Snowflake asked.

"She does," Holly said, "and I think it's a good one. Liz went through her dad's briefcase before we got here tonight and found his notes on the jury selection. She wrote down the names of all the jurors and she went online to get their addresses." Holly handed Snowflake a piece of paper with the information. "Can you check to see if there are any True Believers on the jury?" she asked.

Snowflake did as she was asked on a device she carried in her hand. A few minutes later, she said, "I'm sorry. None of them are True Believers. But they are good people. They only wanted simple gifts as children, never asking for more than they should. And they were well-behaved. They just stopped believing when they got older."

Holly hung her head. "If only I could do magic, maybe I could do something to help."

"Your test is in two days, on your birthday," Snowflake said. "You'll be 35. If you pass, you'll be an elf. Maybe you'll take over my job one day."

"Wait," Liz said, "your birthday is on Christmas Day?"

"All elves are born on Christmas," Holly said. "But I'm not ready, not sure I'll be able to pass the test."

"Why not?" Liz asked. "You're smart."

"She struggles with the math," Snowflake said. "She has everything else down, but to work in the records department, she has to make an A in fifth-grade math."

"I can help with that," Liz said. "Math is one of my best subjects. I have a few shortcuts I can show you. We'll work on it tonight and tomorrow."

"Yes, but even if I pass, it won't be in time to save Twirly," Holly said. "We need to make the jury believe in Twirly before Christmas."

"That's it! You're brilliant, Holly," Liz said. "We do need to make them believe in Twirly. But more importantly, we need make them believe again, just like they did when they were children."

"What do you have in mind, little girl?" Snowflake asked.

When Liz told Snowflake and Holly her plan, Holly said, "Hey, that might work!"

Snowflake looked at Liz and smiled. "You are your father's daughter."

Christmas Eve

9:15 a.m.

Raker sat at counsel table studying his notes while Twirly doodled Christmas trees on a legal pad next to him. Raker could hear Johnson's associates fawning over him, but Sarah's voice wasn't among them. He looked across the aisle and saw her sitting alone, studying her computer screen. Working hard, as always. Hank Snow came in and shook hands with Clyde Driscole and Big Slim. Chip followed him.

"Daddy." Liz leaned over the rail toward him and whispered. "The one with the red hair? He helped

Mr. Snow steal and burn the lease extension."

Raker turned to look at him and then at Liz. He was glad to see her face showed no fear, just the determination her mother used to show when confronted with a challenge.

"Holly and I have something for you, Daddy." Holly was sitting in the first pew next to Liz. She pulled a piece of paper from her front pocket, and handed it across to Raker. When Raker studied it, he saw a layout of the courtroom that included a drawing of the jury box, with 12 squares representing each juror. There also was a square for Cleve R. Johnson, and one for Judge Stark. Fourteen squares in all. Inside each square were two words.

"It's from The Archives," Holly said.

"Daddy, they're the last presents they received before they stopped believing."

Henry Edmonds, who was seated next to Liz, said, "They went to the source, Thad. The information is accurate." Pointing at one of the boxes, Edmonds said, "Save him for last. I have a hunch he will be elected foreman. His dog, Sport, was his constant companion when he was a boy."

Before Raker could respond, Liz said. "Daddy, I want you to know that I still believe. I really do. And I'm sorry I ever doubted. And Daddy, I believe you will win."

Raker felt a lump in his throat. Twelve years earlier at the Edmonds trial, Liz's mother had given Raker the same message. She believed in him. Now his daughter did, too.

"Use that piece of paper, and we will win, Mr. Raker. I just know it," Holly said.

Raker was puzzled at first. He took a moment to study the paper, thinking about The Archives and remembering how it helped save Christmas once before. And then he got it. He knew what he would say to the jury. And while he didn't share Holly's optimism that he could save the property, perhaps he could drive up the price that the county would have to pay.

Liz, Holly and Henry settled back into their seats. Laura, her husband and their two children shared the row with them. Austin Land had assumed his usual corner spot in the back of the courtroom. His laptop was open.

Twirly began to hum a tune. It took Raker a moment to realize it was "Jingle Bells." He wondered why his client was so upbeat. He was about to lose his property on Christmas Eve, and when he did, Christmas in Zone 24 would collapse in a heap of wrecked drones, and belief in Santa Claus would evaporate with the drifting smoke.

Maybe, Raker thought, it was because Twirly sensed that he was starting to believe again; Raker certainly felt it. He knew it was probably too late, but it was something.

Raker heard the courtroom door bang open, followed by the buzz of low voices in the pews. He turned to see who else had arrived. It was a line of small people, all about Hank Snow's size. Some of them strutted, some of them skipped, and some of them pointed to Hank and Chip, giggling as they did. There must have been about 30 of them, happily filling the pews on Twirly's side of the courtroom. At first, Raker thought they were children, but as he looked closer, he noticed their ears. Pointed. And they were dressed in colorful clothes, green trousers, red vests, yellow sashes and the like. Some had small hats made of green felt. Most had shoes that curled at the toes. They had mature faces with youthful dispositions. Raker couldn't believe what he was seeing: three rows of elves.

One more person came in, trailing the elves, carrying a suitcase. She walked down the aisle to Raker's table and asked, "Remember me?"

"Gloria Patten, how could I forget," Raker said. She looked older, of course, but unlike their last meeting, she looked happy and at peace.

"I'll bet you've tried." She laughed.

"I lost that case, not you. You were telling the truth."

"If I were on the jury, I wouldn't have believed me either," Gloria said. "But all's well that ends well. Those little red drones pointed me to my good friend Twirly here, and ever since, life has been one fantastic adventure."

"Thanks for coming, Gloria. But I see you're packed and ready to go once the jury renders the verdict. Probably a good idea."

"Oh, this." She held up the suitcase. "Don't be silly, I'm here to watch a victory. This holds a few delicacies I put together this morning, because your new crowd of supporters can't go long without their snacks. I am hoping this will keep them quiet and attentive."

A few minutes later, at exactly 9:30, Judge Stark entered the courtroom. The elves grew quiet but Raker had the feeling that he could hear their silence. He saw the judge take note of them, tilting his head a bit to one side as if trying to figure them out. Then, true to his nature, Judge Stark got down to business.

The first official act of the day was a jury instruction conference with the lawyers. Johnson's team had submitted standard instructions on what the jury should be told and what it was supposed to decide, which Raker said were fine, but then Johnson asked for more.

"Your honor, the jury should be instructed in no uncertain terms that it cannot consider any evidence — so-called evidence — related to Santa Claus."

"Mr. Johnson," Judge Stark said, "you want me to instruct the jury that there is no such thing as Santa Claus. Is there something you are worried about?"

Cleve R. Johnson puffed out his chest. "I am not the least bit worried, but I want to avoid Mr. Raker turning this case into a referendum on Santa Claus. It's his *modus operandi* and it's the court's duty to cut him off."

"Mr. Johnson, would you like to borrow my robe?"

"Excuse me?" Johnson asked.

"The next time you tell me how to do my job I am sending you to lockup. Are we clear?"

He didn't wait for an answer. "Oh, and by the way, your request is denied. The pattern jury instructions don't mention Santa Claus and I am not about to instruct the jury as to what to think about

elves, reindeer and flying sleighs. Anything else?"
Hearing nothing, he waved the lawyers back to their
seats and told the bailiff to bring in the jury. A few
minutes later, Judge Stark addressed them.

"This is the time of the trial when the lawyers
make their closing arguments. They can summarize
the evidence, but what they say is not evidence. You
are the sole judges of the evidence, not them. I have
cautioned them about spending too much time with
their arguments, reminding them you have listened
to everything and can make up your own minds. But
you know lawyers. They have to talk. So please do
them the courtesy of listening. If they put you to
sleep, it's their fault. But do your best to stay awake."

With that introduction, Judge Stark looked to
Johnson and said, "You're up."

"Your honor," Johnson said. "Ms. Kennedy will
be making the opening remarks. After Mr. Raker
speaks, I will finish up."

"I can't wait," Judge Stark said.

Sarah began with an explanation of condemnation law, breaking it down in a way the jury could
understand. "The county takes private property,"
she said, "only when it is trying to serve the local
residents. Sometimes the property is taken for
roads, sometimes utilities. Sometimes, it is taken to

improve quality of life, like in this case." She admitted that mistakes were made in this case by the county. "But those mistakes do not mean the taking is illegal; it is still for a public purpose."

Sarah was hitting the right points, but Raker thought she sounded sad, as if she'd like to escape. As she concluded her message, she looked at Raker and said, "Mr. Masters deserves to be compensated fairly for his property." Turning back to the jury, she ended by saying, "I want ... I mean ... the county wants you to be fair and just to Mr. Masters in your verdict."

It sounded as if Sarah was pulling for him. Perhaps she believed in the same causes he did. Perhaps her idea of justice was different from that of her boss. He suddenly felt a bond with Sarah he hadn't felt before. She believed in his client, just as he did. Maybe she believed in him, too.

When it was Raker's turn, he started by thanking the jury for their attention during the trial and for performing their civic duty. "Without juries," he explained, "the legal system would be lost, without a compass. Juries sort out truth from deceit." And one more thing, Raker said: "Twirly is fully prepared to accept your verdict; there will be no appeal. He trusts you to do the right thing."

Raker explained that justice is at the foundation of the legal system. "I have the utmost respect for Ms. Kennedy; she is right about the law. So is Judge Stark. It's true. The county can take a man's property and turn it into a park." Raker paused. "But is it justice?" he asked.

"Sometimes, justice is not about what you have the legal right to do but about whether you should do it. People like Clyde Driscole, Big Slim Thompson and Hank Snow use the power of the law to take advantage of others. They've been working with the biggest law firm in the county to make it happen in this case. It's just Twirly Masters and me up against the full force and fury of Johnson, Brakeman & Walker." He gave a short laugh.

"You can't stop the county from taking Twirly's property. I know that. But you do have the power to make the county pay for what it's doing. You determine the price tag for the taking."

He reminded the jury how "fair" the county wanted to be to Twirly. "They want to give him a low-ball sack of coins for property that has been in his family for hundreds of years. There is a saying in this line of work. When the government comes knocking on your door with what it says is a fair deal, it's time to run for cover. Because something is amiss!"

A few jurors smiled. He walked to counsel table, picked up his copy of the verdict sheet and held it up for all see. "You're going to be asked to answer a question on this verdict sheet about the value of the property. To help you make that decision, Judge Stark is going to instruct you on the law. You will hear about a concept known as 'the highest and best use' for property being condemned. When you get to the jury room, I want you to think about that idea very carefully. Think about the highest and best use of Twirly's property on this particular day: Christmas Eve."

Raker then pointed to the elves in the courtroom. He started to say the property is more than a place to work, because real people live there, but caught himself and suppressed a smile. Instead, he said, "Twirly is like a father figure to his employees. Treats them like family. Offers them a place to live, no matter what they look like, or where they come from."

The elves whispered among themselves and smiled at the attention. This was when the jurors looked more closely at the new arrivals sitting in the pews on Twirly's side of the courtroom. Raker noticed the jurors were confused, not by what he said but by what they were seeing. They were looking at small people with pointy ears.

Raker set the verdict sheet on counsel table and reached into his pocket. He pulled out the piece of paper Holly had given him. He glanced over it before continuing.

"Members of the jury," Raker said, "Mr. Johnson is hoping to knock this case out of the park, in order to build a park, like a kid at Christmas playing with a brand new *Louisville Slugger* baseball bat."

The information Holly and Liz had pulled from The Archives showed that an autographed Louisville Slugger baseball bat was the last Christmas present Cleve R. Johnson received as a child before he stopped believing in Santa Claus. Raker wanted to look at Johnson to see if his comment had registered, but dared not. He wanted the jury's attention to be fixed on himself.

Looking again at the piece of paper in his hand, Raker saw the words *BB gun* in the box above Judge Stark's name. He smiled to himself, because it brought back good memories of the judge. "Twirly Masters," he said, "had a lot of fun growing up on the property using a *BB gun* he'd received for Christmas to keep squirrels out of his mother's garden. It was a gift from Santa Claus." A *BB gun* was the Christmas present Judge Stark wanted as a child, but he missed out on it when he stopped believing in Santa Claus. He finally got the gift on Christmas morning after rendering his verdict in the "trial of the century." Raker looked to Judge Stark, who nodded in return.

Raker continued with the theme. "Twirly's family and helpers have been doing important work for Santa Claus for many years, centuries in fact. They have brought Christmas joy to millions and millions of children."

While he looked at juror 5, he mentioned the fun of playing with a new *yo-yo* on Christmas morning. When he looked at juror 9, he talked about the imaginary world brought to life by a *Barbie doll*. With juror 3, it was the comfort of a cuddly *Teddy bear*. It was all about twirling around in a *hula-hoop* with juror 7. And so on. Each time he mentioned two words from the paper in his hand, he felt he was making a connection with a juror.

When Raker got to the last juror, a man in his early 70s, he looked him in the eye. "Nothing lasts forever," Raker said. "Like a *puppy dog*. We want him to be a friend for life. But life isn't fair that way. I have a dog, Comet. He sleeps with my daughter, watches over her, loves her, and she loves him, but one day he'll grow old and die. I suppose that's the message the county is sending. Out with the old, in with the new. Don't sweat it, Mr. Masters. It's just a piece of land. It's just a *puppy dog*. You can buy another one."

Raker paused, but he continued to look the man in the eye, hoping for that spark of understanding. When the man reached up with his shirt-sleeve to wipe an eye, he knew he'd done the best he could.

Raker put the piece of paper back in his pocket and looked around the courtroom. When he did, he felt his spirts lifted by the family and friends who were there to support him. When he looked into the eyes of Henry Edmonds, he felt courage. The face of Twirly Masters made him optimistic. His daughter, Liz, and sister, Laura, made him feel loved. Looking at Holly, he felt determined. The collection of elves left him with hope; they were ready to make Christmas possible for the children of Christmas Zone 24. And with Sarah Kennedy, Raker felt young again, ready to tackle the world and try new things. With all of them, Raker felt united in spirit. He envisioned an ending to the trial with happy children on Christmas morning. He now knew his purpose for being there. He was standing where he was needed most, in a courtroom on Christmas Eve with a chance to save Christmas, as he had done once before. He turned back to the jury and spoke to them as if they were family.

"Mr. Masters lives in a special place," Raker said. "It's special to him and to those who live and work with him. It's special to the children who depend upon his generous spirit at this time of year. And it's special to the adults in this world who, like you, will find it in their hearts to believe again, on Christmas Eve, just as you did when you were children."

Raker looked at the jurors one last time. "Thank you for listening. I hope each of you has a very Merry Christmas."

When Raker was through, Johnson stood up and walked to the center of the courtroom. "Members of the jury," he began, "this is a real case. It is not make-believe." Without hesitating, he attacked Masters for not taking the county's offer of $100,000; it is more than fair, he said, and his refusal to take it shows his greed. "That's one of the problems with the legal system today: opportunists looking for a handout."

But Johnson didn't end with his personal attack on Masters. He jumped on Raker as well. "Santa Claus and Mr. Raker must be related," he said, "because he and his clients mention Santa Claus in all their Christmas trials. It's a waste of your time and an insult to your intelligence."

After belittling Masters and Raker, Johnson told the jury that his law firm had handled hundreds of condemnation cases for local governments. "I have never seen a property owner with a case so weak or so poorly handled."

None of these remarks were proper, because Johnson was not a witness and not allowed to give evidence. Raker just listened and trusted. He let Johnson keep digging and digging. Pretty soon, Raker hoped, the hole would be 6 feet deep.

Johnson then defended the appraisal. In doing so, he criticized Raker for questioning the experience and qualifications of Lori Lannigan. "She has three times the number of professional degrees he does, and was doing appraisals when he was in nursery school. Calling her 'Low-Ball' is an insult."

Raker suppressed a smile. He was glad Johnson had reminded the jury of her nickname.

Johnson then spoke of Big Slim Thompson in a tone of reverence that he might have used in reference to the Founding Fathers. "He's just the kind of man you want on your side: a bold thinker, a man of vision, a man who builds things for his community. A man who won in a landslide in the November election."

Raker noticed two of the jurors smirking. Perhaps they were thinking about the campaign contribution from North Pole Enterprises.

After taking a few seconds to catch his breath, Johnson said, "Now let's talk about the other side's theory in this case." Johnson's next words made it clear that he was disgusted with the claim that the county was in league with an evil man who works for Santa Claus. "Mr. Masters had to be drinking his fair share of eggnog to come up with that tale. All this talk about drones delivering presents for Santa Claus is silly. The next thing you know, the Easter Bunny will be using automated pogo sticks to deliver colored eggs."

Johnson then nodded to one of his associates, who pushed a button on his computer that brought up a photo of the entire property on the courtroom monitors. "This is not science fiction," Johnson said. "What you see is what you get. It's just 90 acres of land, with an old house and a few run-down buildings. Not exactly Santa's playground. If you use your imaginations, I'll bet you can dream up anything about the property, just as Mr. Masters did, to try to prevent the county from building a park." Johnson joked that perhaps the county should not take the land "because it will close down the earth-based refueling center for the Starship Enterprise. Unidentified flying objects. Really," he sniffed.

Raker watched the jury closely. His gut told him the jurors favored Twirly Masters and the Haints over the scheming of the county and the rhetoric of Cleve R. Johnson, but he was concerned, because the jury had limited power in the case. Even if they set a higher price than the county's appraiser suggested, the county would deliver the check and the sheriff would escort everyone from the property.

As Raker was thinking about the problem facing his client and the risk to Christmas, Johnson finished up. He thanked the jury for their attention and praised them with a parting shot: "I am confident you have the intelligence and common sense to do the right thing."

Raker hoped Johnson was right.

Christmas Eve

10:45 a.m.

For the next 30 minutes, Judge Stark instructed the jury on the law and what they had to do. He explained to them that the county had the right to take private property for a public park, but the county had to pay just compensation, and that's where they came in.

"You must decide the fair market value of the property as of the date of the taking, which is today. In arriving at the fair market value, you are allowed to consider the highest and best use of the property as of today."

"You are the sole judges of what is true and what is not. You can believe all, some or none of what any witness has said in this case. In determining whether to believe a witness, you should use the same tests of truthfulness that you use in your everyday lives. You also may consider the opinion of an expert witness, but you are not bound by it. Finally, if you determine that a witness is interested in the outcome of the case, you may take that interest into account."

Raker looked at Johnson and thought about his lineup of interested witnesses, including Lori "Low-Ball" Lannigan, Big Slim Thompson and the chief operating officer of North Pole Enterprises, Hank Snow.

"In deciding this case, you must be persuaded, considering all the evidence, that your verdict is more likely than not to be correct. You may not speculate about the fair market value of the property, nor may you base your decision on imaginative uses for the property."

Raker knew that Judge Stark was going to give this instruction, but he was worried, because he was depending on the imagination of the jury.

"When you go back into the jury room, you must pick your foreman and then answer the one question on the verdict sheet. Just fill in the number on the sheet to let us know the fair market value of Mr. Masters' property. Your verdict must be unanimous."

Judge Stark called the lawyers to the bench and asked them if there were any objections to his instructions. Hearing none, he sent the jury out to do their duty. After the jury was gone, he said, "The court will be at ease while the jury deliberates."

Raker looked at the clock. It was 11:15 a.m. Behind him, he heard something ping. Then he heard it again. He turned around to see Henry Edmonds looking at a device in his hand. "What have you got there, Henry?" Raker asked.

"You remember that little flash drive computer from my trial?"

"How could I forget?" Raker said. "It's the reason you were on trial."

"In the last 12 years, we've made some improvements in the technology used by collectors. At the time of my trial, this device could tell me within seconds about a change in the behavior of children on the Naughty and Nice lists. However, it could not tell me in real-time about changes in The Archives. Now it does."

"How does it work?"

"A 'ping' indicates there has been a change for a person in my district. One tone tells me that a child has moved from the Naughty list to the Nice list. Another tone notifies me that a child may be getting coal in his stocking unless he turns things around in time. The tone you just heard tracks something very special."

"And what's that?" Raker asked.

"Whenever you hear that tone, it means that an adult listed in The Archives has become a True Believer."

Raker laughed. "You mean like in the movie 'It's A Wonderful Life' where the little girl tells her dad that every time a bell rings, an angel gets its wings?"

"Very good, Thad," Edmonds said. "We think of True Believers as being like angels. They keep the spirit of Christmas alive for all generations."

Just then, the device pinged again. "What's the range on that thing?" Raker asked.

"Right now, I have it set to measure activity in the jury room."

While Raker was thinking about the significance of that comment, Edmonds got up and walked a few feet to meet Judge Stark, who had come down from the bench. Raker stayed put but he could hear the conversation.

"How are you doing, Mr. Edmonds?" Judge Stark asked. "It's been a long time since you've been in my courtroom."

"Trying to behave myself, your honor."

"I have a letter here," Judge Stark said. "I wonder if you'd be kind enough to deliver it for me."

"With great pleasure!"

When Edmonds returned to his seat, Raker asked, "What was that about?"

"Oh, this?" Edmonds looked at the letter and smiled. "He's a True Believer, Thad. Thought you knew that. He's been writing to Santa Claus every year for the last twelve years."

Raker was trying to absorb this news when he was distracted by Sarah Kennedy; she stood up and asked Judge Stark for permission to address the court.

"What's it about, Ms. Kennedy?" Judge Stark asked.

"May it please the court, your honor, I request permission to withdraw as counsel for the county, effective immediately."

"I object." Cleve R. Johnson sounded as shocked as Raker felt.

"Mr. Johnson," Judge Stark said, "I have a feeling that if your wife wanted a divorce, you would file a motion to contest it. Sit down, and let me hear from Ms. Kennedy."

"Your honor," Kennedy said. "I waited until the jury was deliberating to make this motion to avoid prejudicing my client, but I don't feel I can continue to represent the county."

Johnson leaned toward Kennedy and muttered, in a voice loud enough for Raker to hear, that she was fired.

"Don't bother," Raker heard her say. "I quit."

"Ms. Kennedy," Judge Stark said, "I see you have your differences with Mr. Johnson, which is understandable. That being said, it is with regret that I allow you to excuse yourself from the county's dream team of lawyers, because 95 percent of the team's brainpower will walk out of the room with you. But I am sure you have your reasons. Motion allowed."

Sarah Kennedy gathered her belongings and walked down the aisle. Raker stood and walked out behind her. When they entered the hallway, she turned to face him.

"Thad, I know how hard you've worked on this case, and I'm sorry I had any part in opposing your efforts. Your closing argument tugged at my heart. I don't want to be sitting there with Cleve and his team of yes-men when Twirly Masters loses his property."

"Funny thing," Raker said, "but Twirly is not worried. Henry is optimistic, too. Maybe they know something I don't. Anyway, it's not your fault. You were just doing your job and it took real courage to withdraw, even at the last minute. I respect you for it."

Just then Liz came out of the courtroom and pulled Sarah and her father together so she could hug them both at the same time.

"What are you doing, Liz?" Raker asked, feeling a bit embarrassed.

"I am hugging two of my three favorite people. We can't forget Aunt Laura," Liz said.

"Thank you, Liz," Sarah said. "That is very kind. I want you to know I won't forget you."

"What do you mean?" Liz asked.

"I'm going to have to move. After what I did in court today, no law firm in this county will hire me."

"You can't leave," Liz pleaded. "Daddy, tell her she needs to stay."

"Give me just a minute, Liz," Raker said. Holly was waiting at the courtroom door, so Liz ran to her and the two of them went back into the courtroom to wait.

"So this is it. You're pulling up stakes?" Raker asked.

"Not sure I have much choice," Sarah said.

"What if I gave you two choices?"

"What do you have in mind?"

Raker laid out his plan, giving her two important things to think about. "Will you at least think about them?" he asked.

Before Sarah could respond, Edmonds stuck his head out the courtroom door. "The jury will be back soon."

"How do you know that?" Raker asked.

Edmonds held up his device. "Eleven pings."

"You're telling me there are now 11 True Believers in the jury room?"

PING!

"Make that 12," Edmonds said. "We'd better get back to the courtroom."

Raker looked at Sarah.

"I will think about your offers," she said. "Let's go hear what the jury has to say first."

Raker hugged her. This time he was not tentative.

When everyone was seated, but before Judge Stark brought the jury back, he made it clear that he wanted no outbursts when the jury announced its verdict.

The jury filed in and took their seats. They didn't look at Cleve R. Johnson, or his remaining team of lawyers. They did look at Twirly Masters and with kindly expressions. Raker held his breath, closed his eyes and believed.

"Ladies and gentlemen," the judge said, "have you reached a verdict?"

The foreman — the man who had loved the puppy named Sport — stood and said they had. The bailiff walked over, retrieved the verdict sheet and handed it to Judge Stark. He looked at it and displayed no emotion. He then handed it to the clerk and asked her to take the verdict.

"Members of the jury," the clerk said. "Please rise."

After all the jurors were standing, she asked them, "In the matter of the county versus Twirly Masters, is it your unanimous verdict that the just compensation to Mr. Masters for the taking of his property is . . ."

The clerk looked hard at the piece of paper in front of her, and she put her finger on the page. She moved it slowly from left to right. Her lips were moving as if she were counting to herself. She looked over at Judge Stark, who nodded at her to proceed.

". . . That the just compensation is one trillion dollars?"

In unison, the jurors answered, "Yes!"

The courtroom was deathly quiet. Raker's head was spinning. Twirly Masters was smiling that bright energetic smile that guided his spirit.

Judge Stark thanked the jurors for their service, said he hoped all their Christmas wishes came true, and they left through the side door of the courtroom. When they were gone, Johnson was on his feet. "This is an outrage, your honor."

"I agree," Judge Stark said, "it seems kind of low to me. By the way, does the county plan to make that deposit with the clerk of court today as you promised?"

"You know very well the county doesn't have that kind of money," Johnson shouted.

"But just to be sure, why don't you talk it over with the county manager and Big Slim. I'll give you a moment."

"I don't have to." Then, in a booming voice that bounced off the courtroom walls, he said, "Your honor, we demand that the court throw out this ridiculously high verdict! It does not conform to the evidence in this case."

"Did you say 'demand'?" Judge Stark asked.

"How about this? Why don't you pick the phrase that best sums up where you and I stand at the moment? This will be multiple choice: Is it A, the last straw? Or B, your swan song? Or C, your last mulligan? Or D, the fat lady has sung? Take your time." Judge Stark nodded to the bailiff who had walked over to position himself behind Johnson.

"You should have stayed retired," Johnson said.

"Cleve R Johnson, Esquire," Judge Stark said, "you are being held in contempt of court for violating all 10 of my rules of court."

"You can't make up rules of court and hold me in contempt for violating them." Johnson's face was becoming pale; it looked constricted by the veins popping in his neck. "The Judicial Standards Commission," he shouted, "will hear about this."

Judge Stark shook his head. "Mr. Johnson, I am sitting here in an emergency capacity only. Judge Davidson should be healed up after Christmas, and the court system won't need me for a while, if at all. I really don't care if you call the Judicial Standards Commission, the governor, the president of the United States or the Supreme Court. I'll be at home watching House Hunters International with my wife."

"Preposterous!"

"Bailiff," Judge Stark said, "take Mr. Johnson into custody."

"Hold still," the young bailiff said. "I'm still trying to get the hang of these things." As the bailiff was locking Johnson's wrists together, Judge Stark began his sermon.

"The problem with you, Mr. Johnson, is that you've come to believe the press releases you pay your publicist to put out about you. My rules of court are not official, but they are universal. They are guidelines for how to behave in life as well as in a courtroom. You didn't listen when you were a young lawyer. Now that you are shackled, perhaps they will sink in. As soon as you can repeat the rules to the magistrate, you will be free to go. So listen well:

"Rule 1: Show up on time. I believe we covered that on the first day.

"Rule 2: Be prepared. Preparation is the key to success. Not brains. Not wisdom. Not oratory. Not experience. Not grades. Not good looks. The only thing that saved your bacon in this trial was Sarah Kennedy, but even she got fed up with you. The next four rules are self-explanatory. You violated all of them.

"Rule 3: Be courteous.

"Rule 4: Don't interrupt.

"Rule 5: Speak clearly.

"Rule 6: Don't be pretentious."

Judge Stark took off his glasses and polished them with his shirt-sleeve. "Violating the next rule cost you the case. Rule 7: Pick your battles. You fought the wrong battle when you made fun of people who believe in Santa Claus."

Cleve R. Johnson was fuming but the bailiff's hand on his shoulder was firm.

"Just three more rules," Judge Stark said. "Hang in there:

"Rule 8: Be a good listener and think before you speak. Humans have two ears and one mouth for a reason. Listen first. Talk third. Think hard in between.

"Rule 9: If you don't have the answer, don't pretend. Juries have an innate ability to detect BS. They figured you out early in this case.

"Rule 10: Maintain your credibility. Since you are in shackles, I am pretty sure you didn't adhere to Rule 10."

After Johnson was shuffled from the courtroom, one of the young lawyers on the county's team stood up and asked if he could have a moment to speak with his client. The judge nodded, and the young man, Big Slim and Clyde Driscole began a heated but indecipherable conversation. Hank Snow left the courtroom with Chip trotting behind him. Henry Edmonds got up and followed them. Everyone else stayed put and appeared to be mesmerized.

A few minutes later, the young lawyer addressed the court again. "Your honor, the county would like to dismiss this case prior to final judgment being entered."

"So the county doesn't want to buy Mr. Masters' property after all?"

"No, your honor."

"But what about the county's contract with North Pole Enterprises?"

"Null and void," Big Slim shouted from the pew behind his lawyer. "If Snow wants to sue, let him try."

"I thank you for clarifying the county's position," the judge said. "but the county seems to have forgotten that Mr. Raker just obtained the biggest condemnation verdict ever recorded in this state. His client now owns this county."

Looking at Big Slim, he added, "Mr. Masters may clean house on the county commission." Judge Stark looked at Clyde Driscole. "Some county employees may need to look for alternate employment, too."

"Your honor," Raker said, "may my client address the court?"

"Sure," Judge Stark replied. "He runs the place now. He can say whatever he wants."

Twirly stood up and smiled at the judge. "Your honor, I want to thank this court for the fine way in which this proceeding was conducted. I've never been a party in a court case before and it was thoroughly delightful. Yes, just delightful. I admit that things didn't look good for me at times, but I was taught at a young age never to give up hope. I just kept telling myself I needed to believe. I believed in my attorney. I believed in the judicial system. And I believed, most of all, in what is about to happen."

"Meaning, you believe in the magic of Christmas?" Judge Stark asked.

The elves began to jabber excitedly and the judge gave them a moment before he gaveled them back into order. "I'd hate to jail you folks on Christmas Eve, with all the work you have to do tonight, but I need to be able to hear Mr. Masters." They quieted quickly, letting out one or two more squeaks.

Twirly smiled at the elves and looked back at the judge. "What you asked me, Judge," Twirly said.

"Yes, I do believe in everything that is magical about Christmas."

Judge Stark's face revealed a sly smile. "What do you want to do about the county's offer? It's either one trillion dollars or your land off Highway 11. One trillion dollars can go a long way."

"Christmas should be a time for joy," Twirly said. He walked over to the clerk and asked for the verdict sheet. Turning around and looking at the county's side of the courtroom, he said, "I hope each of you has a very Merry Christmas!" He crumbled the verdict sheet into a ball, covered it with both hands and rubbed his hands together. When he opened his hands for all to see, the verdict sheet had disappeared.

"Are you saying you want to keep the property?" Judge Stark asked.

"Yes, sir," Masters said.

"And you want to let the county keep the one trillion dollars it doesn't have?"

"My Christmas gift," Twirly said.

"Why?" Judge Stark asked.

Twirly smiled. "Because tomorrow is a very special day and there is a lot of work to do at the Haints tonight."

The elves in the courtroom cheered as they hopped out of their seats and scampered to form two lines, one on each side of the courtroom aisle. As Holly stepped forward to greet Twirly, the elves started singing a Christmas song. It was Twirly's favorite. Holly put her baseball cap on her head and slid the bill just a bit to the right, smiling at Big Slim Thompson and Clyde Driscole as she did. Twirly then clasped her hand, and, together, they walked between the boisterous elves and out the courtroom door, laughing all the way.

Christmas Eve

12:30 p.m.

Raker was the only one left in the courtroom; he was enjoying a quiet moment of reflection after the verdict was handed down. The property was saved and Christmas would come, but he was anxious, because there was something on his mind. Or rather, there was someone on his mind. Sarah had not responded to either of his offers.

"Are you going to sit here all day, basking in your glory?"

Raker turned to see Sarah standing in the back of the courtroom, smiling. He stood up and walked to her, grasping both her hands in his.

"Let's go to the second floor," she said. "I think there's an application we need to complete and a fee we need to pay."

Raker was exuberant, but his mood was interrupted by the buzz of his cellphone. When he saw who it was, he said, "Excuse me, just one second. Don't go anywhere."

"We have a problem, Thad," Edmonds said.

"What is it?"

"While everyone was in court this morning, Snow had a crew from the North Pole come to the Haints."

"And do what?" Raker waited.

"All the presents. They've been removed from the house."

"What do you mean, they've been removed?"

"I suspected Snow was up to something based on a conversation I overhead between him and his helper, Chip," Edmonds said. "So I followed them when they left the courtroom after the verdict and they led me to where I am standing now."

"Where is that?"

"Outside the storage building on Twirly's property. The presents are inside."

"So that's good, right?" Raker asked.

"No. They're locked in the mechanical arms of thousands of little red drones, stacked from floor to ceiling in an open area of the storage building."

"Can't Twirly and his elves take the presents back, now that you've found them?"

"No, they are locked up tight, and the clock is ticking. They have built-in timers that have them scheduled to lift off tonight."

"Can't you disable the system?"

"I've been trying. They are connected remotely to a computer enclosed in a case attached to the wall. I was able to break the lock on the case and access the computer, but I have no computer skills. I don't know what to do. Twirly is on his way, but he says his people aren't equipped to handle this either. His technology department was outsourced as part of Snow's changes and is under Snow's control. Do you have any ideas, Thad? Because if you don't, all your good work will have been wasted."

Sarah was looking at Raker with a concerned expression on her face. Raker, thinking, stopped talking for a moment. Then he had an idea. "Henry, give me an hour. I'll meet you at the property."

When he hung up, Sarah asked, "Is everything OK?"

"No, but hold on just a second." He looked at his phone again and dialed another number.

"Judy Robertson," the voice answered.

"Judy, it's me, Thad."

"Thad, I heard the news. Congratulations!"

"Thanks, but we have a problem. Do you think you could use the computer skills you used 12 years ago to save Christmas, again?"

When Judy asked for an explanation, Raker gave it, and she was eager to help. He told her where to meet him, hung up the phone and looked Sarah in the eye.

"I have to go to the Haints. We have a crisis. But I'm not going anywhere until we make that stop on the second floor. Are you ready?"

Christmas Eve

4:00 p.m

When Raker first saw the scene, it looked like the setting for a futuristic movie. Little red drones filled the entire football-field-sized storage area and were stacked 20 high. They were blinking and buzzing, as if they were itching to take off. The roof of the building had been removed, opening a wide path to the sky above.

The mainframe computer where Judy Robertson's talents had been focused for the past two hours had an electronic counter on it, displaying just 120 minutes until liftoff. Raker felt helpless. He couldn't argue his way to victory in this place. Success depended on an understanding of technology that he didn't possess.

Twirly's elves had been hard at work trying to remove the presents from the drones, but the same system powering the drones to countdown and liftoff appeared to control the release of the presents. They were not coming loose unless Judy was able to override the system.

Raker and Masters stood to one side, giving Judy space to do her work, when Holly and Liz walked up.

"How's it going, Mr. Raker?" Holly asked.

"Judy has gotten through the first two layers of security and is working on the last. This one is more difficult, she says, because it is triggered by a password."

"Maybe we can help," Liz said. "After all, we figured out Twirly's system."

Twirly laughed. "Jingle all the way."

"If you have any ideas, I am sure she would welcome them," Raker said.

"It's all about trying to think like the person who set the password," Holly said.

"She's right, Daddy," Liz said. "We need to think like Hank Snow."

"Then we need to be devious. And right sneaky. Yes, indeed," Masters said.

"So," Raker said, "if you were Hank Snow and you wanted to set a password that described yourself in six letters, what would you select?"

"How about Grinch?" Holly asked. Everyone laughed.

Just then, one of the drones on a tall stack in the middle of the storage building began to make odd sounds and it lifted into the air. As Raker and the others looked up, it passed overhead and flew toward the front of the building. They all ran to follow, onto the front porch and into the yard where Liz said Snow burned the lease extension. They stopped and looked up. Raker didn't see the drone, but he could hear it, somewhere high, up near the treetops.

From across the yard, near the edge of the woods, Raker saw Edmonds walk out, pulling Chip along by the ear. "I found him hiding at the stable," Edmonds said.

"Does he know anything?" Twirly asked.

"Nothing he will admit to," Edmonds said.

Chip stopped in front of Raker and crossed his arms. "You won't win this time, Raker. Mr. Snow has beaten you."

As Raker thought about what he might do to convince Chip to come clean, he could still hear the buzzing high above him. The machine was hovering.

"Chip," Raker said, "do you realize that you are a conspirator in a crime?"

"Nice try," Chip said. "The presents belong to North Pole Enterprises and Mr. Snow is the highest local authority for the company. It's not stealing to take your own property."

"Ah," Raker said, "but it is a crime when you trespass on someone else's property to do your dirty work. You conspired with Hank Snow to do it on Twirly's property."

"How many years in jail for that?" Edmonds asked Raker.

"Depends on the judge," Raker said. "I think we have time to get Chip an audience in front of Judge Stark next week before he retires again."

Chip's confidence disappeared, and he made a run for it. His sudden motion triggered something in the loose drone. Like an animal that senses its prey is trying to escape, it took off. The noise it made grew louder as the bright red Vesta swooped down past Raker's ear and leveled off in pursuit of Chip. It gained ground quickly and knocked Chip off his feet before it went high into the air to swing around and make another pass, like a fighter plane after a slow moving target on open water. Chip stood up, 50 yards away from Raker's group, and yelled, "Help me."

As the drone reached the highest point in its arc and was preparing to make another pass at Chip, Raker said, "You help us, Chip, and we'll help you."

"OK, OK, I'll help you," Chip screamed, his arms up to protect his head.

"Then I suggest you run hard, Chip, and follow us."

As the drone started its descent, the sound of its motor revved up. Raker, Masters, Edmonds, Liz and Holly took off for the front door. Chip hustled to catch up. On the front steps of the porch, Holly tripped and fell as the others made it through the door. Raker was holding the door for everyone so he could slam it shut on the drone, when he saw Chip step on Holly and push her back to the ground before he came up the steps and through the door. Holly stood up, dazed. The drone was heading for the door at high speed, and she was in the direct path. Raker felt Liz beside him and then he felt her move.

"Shut the door behind me, Daddy," she yelled.

Seconds before the drone was about to smash into Holly's head, Liz threw her body into her, tackling her to the ground. The drone sailed over their heads and crashed into the door just closed by Raker, splintering it to pieces. The machine hit the floor, slid to a stop, coughed once and, just before it died, the arms holding the presents sprang open.

Raker stepped through the broken door and ran to the girls, followed by Edmonds and Masters. He knelt beside Liz and Holly. "Is everyone OK?" he asked.

Liz and Holly said nothing at first. They were twisted together in a heap on the ground. Slowly, with Raker's help, they began to unwind themselves until they could sit up next to one another. They had dirt-streaked faces, mixed with a little blood from the cuts on their foreheads. When they looked at each other, they began to laugh at the same time. They couldn't stop for the next two minutes.

"Well," Edmonds said, "that will be a story you can tell for years to come."

Masters had a look of admiration on his face. "Spectacular," he said, "Yes, spectacular, indeed!"

After the crash, Judy appeared at the front of the building, looking surprised by the broken door, the smoking drone and the bodies on the ground.

"It's OK," Raker said. "They're fine."

Chip followed her out and stood on the porch. And then they heard it: The humming from the drones inside the building stopped. "Did you disable them?" Raker asked.

"No," Judy said. "I don't know what happened."

"I do," Chip said. "It's the defect in the system. One fails, they all fail."

Raker stepped past Judy and ran into the open storage area. There was nothing but silence. He looked at the stacks of drones and noticed that the arms that held the presents in place had retracted.

Now it was just a matter of separating the good presents from the bad machines.

Christmas Eve

8:45 p.m.

Liz loved the Christmas Eve traditions with her dad: first, the 6:00 o'clock candles and carols service at the small church where her parents were married, then Aunt Laura's house for dinner and now the outdoor skating rink. Raker told her, her mother had loved to skate as a child, and so did she, especially on Christmas Eve.

Liz was quick to lace up and hit the ice, while Raker took a seat at a bench on the side. She glided across the ice under the stars for more than 30 minutes. She was happy. She was excited. It was almost Christmas. When she came to a stop in the middle of the rink, she tilted her head back and took one last look at the vast sky above. It was a beautiful night. A quiet night. A silent, peaceful night, just like in the song they sang in church. And then she saw it, a streaking spark that left a smoke-like stream in its wake, like that from of a high-flying jet. Liz smiled. She knew it wasn't a jet. And she knew where the streaking object was headed. Twirly and Holly lived in that direction.

When they pulled into their driveway around 9:45, the first thing Liz noticed was the Christmas tree in their living-room window. The colored lights shone and twinkled; it was their welcome home — that and the excited barking of Comet. Liz got out of the car and ran to the house to greet him.

Raker followed her and went into the kitchen to get a glass of water. He saw an envelope addressed to him on the kitchen table, with a return address that said, "North Pole." Nothing else. Inside the envelope, Raker found a folded card that had a drawing of a snowflake on the front. The handwritten note began, "Hello, kind sir. I'm glad I could help, but it was you who saved Christmas."

Raker stopped and thought. It was the second time Snowflake had used the confidential information from The Archives to help Raker win the day. In the first trial, The Archives had revealed Judge Stark's childhood wish for a BB gun. In this trial, it provided the personal information needed to persuade the jurors to save Christmas. The note ended by saying, "Merry Christmas to you and to your new family!"

Raker's eyes welled up. Snowflake had been watching out for him all along. As had Henry. His friends at the North Pole had not abandoned him, as he had thought for so long. They had always been there. They had always believed in him, no matter how little he believed in return. He tucked the note in his pocket and walked to Liz's room to tuck her in, too.

When Raker got to Liz's room, she was sitting in bed, the covers pulled up to her waist. Her blond hair was not as curly as it had been when she was 4 years old, but it still flowed freely to her shoulders.

Comet's muzzle was gray and grizzled now. He curled up at the end of Liz's bed every night, and when he saw Raker come into the room, his tail began to wag.

"Daddy," she said. "Tell me the story again!"

"What?" Raker said. Then he remembered their old routine. "But you've heard the story more times than you can count."

Liz knew the drill, too. She pleaded again, with her smile mostly, and when that didn't work, she said, "Oh, please, Daddy, just one more time!"

As he had done when she was younger, he sat down on her bed and squeezed her tight. "You are such a little mess."

"Daddy," she whispered, both arms around his neck. "I know I'm a little mess, but tell me the story again. Tell me how I got my name."

"You know very well how you got your name."

"I know, Daddy, but I like to hear you tell it. Please!"

Raker went to the closet and found her old Mickey Mouse night light. He plugged it in and turned off her bedside lamp, leaving only the soft glow from the corner of the room. Then, as he had done countless times when Liz was younger, he crawled over Comet, put his arm around her and began.

"Elizabeth Henry Raker, you were named after two very special people. You know the man now; he's Henry Edmonds, who at great risk to his freedom, went on trial 12 years ago to save Christmas. The other was your mother, Elizabeth, who believed in the goodness of people, in hope, in charity, but most of all, she found a way to believe in me even when I didn't believe in myself." Raker wiped at his eye. He ended the story by saying: "She would have loved you very much."

"Thank you, Daddy."

"You're very welcome." Kissing her on her head, Raker said, "Sleep tight."

"Don't let the bed bugs bite." She sat up and gave him another hug. "Good night, Daddy. I love you."

"I love you more," Raker said. "Merry Christmas!"

Austin Land was up late on Christmas Eve to finish his exclusive exposé. He sat in a dimly lit corner of a large newsroom. Everyone else who worked at the newspaper was at home with family. The final edition had been put to bed. On nights like this, Land liked to pass his time at the keyboard to avoid reminding himself of his choice to remain single. It made him feel less lonely to tell stories.

With the details provided by Twirly Masters, the research he had done and the action he witnessed firsthand in the courtroom, he had put together the makings of a journalistic masterpiece. If he pitched it to the right media outlets, it could be highly successful; the fame might even lead to a book deal.

It was the story of a trial in three parts, covering a period of 12 years. He dubbed it, "The Trial of Thad Raker." Part I was the Edmonds trial, when Raker saved Christmas and became a True Believer. In Part II, Raker lost his way and his belief in Christmas due to family tragedy and the Patten trial. But in Part III, the Masters trial, Raker not only saved Christmas again, he saved himself.

As Austin Land put the finishing touches on his work, he realized he had to make a decision. The publicity from the story might be a problem for Twirly Masters. Land could envision the property becoming overrun with tourists, conspiracy theorists, and child-welfare officers wanting to examine the elves' birth certificates. Government officials and the military might involve themselves in investigating the strange object landing and taking off at the Haints every Christmas Eve. If Land published the story, he could be the one to put Christmas at risk.

As he sat there ruminating, he thought back to his conversation with Twirly Masters earlier that day. Masters admitted that Land's article could hurt Christmas, but he said he was honoring their deal. "You came through for us," Masters said. "Yes, you did. Heck of a reporter, you are. Just the best. Don't you worry about a thing. I have to be true to myself. It's more important to keep my word to you."

Land wondered why Masters had talked about being true to himself. And then Land had a feeling; he hadn't felt this way in a long time. He needed to be true to himself, too.

He looked out the window and saw that it had begun to snow. He felt like he did as a boy on Christmas Eve when he still believed.

Turning back to his computer screen, he looked one last time at the story, the best thing he'd ever written. His finger hovered and, with a sigh, he touched the delete key. The story — along with potential fame — was gone for good.

At the same moment that Austin Land hit the delete key on his computer, a device pinged in Henry Edmonds' pocket. It had that special tone.

Edmonds smiled. Austin Land was now a True Believer. Way to go, Austin, and a very Merry Christmas to you!

KENNEDY & RAKER

ATTORNEYS AT LAW

Epilogue

Christmas Day

4:30 p.m.

The gathering at Raker's law office was spur-of-the-moment, but then again, life had been moving at a rapid pace the past four days.

Raker and Liz arrived first and had just finished arranging the furniture in the conference room when Laura, her husband and two little boys came through the front door. She hugged her brother and, in the sarcastic tone that had become his emotional support for the past decade, said, "It's about time you got around to this, little brother. You look nice. Are you ready?"

"I am, but I'm worried about Liz. It's always been just her and me."

Laura scoffed. "She practically put this together single-handedly."

"I can hear you, Daddy, and she's right," Liz said. "It's time you were happy again."

The conference table had been pushed to one corner and chairs arranged around the room. Liz had placed pots of poinsettias on the table.

Judy Robertson and her husband, Jason Peabody, arrived, and Judy rushed to give Raker a hug. Peabody stuck out his hand and pulled Raker in for a man-hug.

Twirly Masters arrived next, with Holly in tow. Holly was not wearing her usual baseball hat. She had a proud smile on her face.

"Daddy," Liz said, "Holly passed her elf test. Look."

Raker looked at Holly and did notice a difference, as she moved her head from left to right, like it was on a swivel. "Pointed ears," Raker said. "Congratulations!"

"Thanks to Liz," Holly said. "I aced the math with her help. And I've been assigned to The Archives to work as Snowflake's assistant."

"She couldn't ask for a more industrious helper," Raker said.

Liz and Holly made eye contact, smiled at each other and ran off. Twirly laughed and moved toward Raker.

"You are one fine-looking husband-in-waiting," Twirly said. "I don't know how you did it, Thad, but I have to say, I knew you could. All the decisions you've made this week, including the one that brought us here today, have been right on target. Yes, right on target. Congratulations!"

"Thank you, Twirly. I learned a lot from you," Raker said. Then he saw that his best man had arrived.

"Glad you could be here, Henry," Raker said. "It means a lot to me."

"Not to worry," Edmonds told him. "I wouldn't miss this for anything."

Laura then took charge. She thanked everyone for coming to this very special occasion on such short notice. She positioned Raker and Henry in the center of the room. When they were in place, Raker saw Holly make quick movements with her hands, causing a string quartet of elves playing classical music to appear in the corner of the room. Raker smiled at her.

A moment later, Liz came through the conference room door carrying a bouquet of flowers. Sarah Kennedy followed close behind. She wore a knee-length white dress and a big smile. Raker doubted that he'd ever smiled wider than he was at that moment. Sarah was beautiful. And smart. And kind. He was a lucky man.

Only one person was missing, the officiant. But Raker knew there was one minute to spare, so he was not worried.

Sure enough, precisely at 5:00 p.m., a distinguished man and lovely woman stood at the conference room door. The man tossed the expensive Rolex watch once owned by Cleve R. Johnson, Esquire, at Raker and said, "Merry Christmas. I thought you would like a memento from the trial. And, by the way, the thing really does work."

Raker caught it and took a deep breath. Augustus Langhorne Stark had arrived, along with his loving wife, Kay. The wedding could proceed.

The room became quiet as Judge Stark took his position in front of the happy couple. He cleared his throat. "Before we get started, I have something to say. This man and this woman are two of the most skilled and honest lawyers in the county, who work hard to do the best they can for their clients. They will be tough to beat following their merger. And I'm not talking about this ceremony."

As if on cue, Twirly and Holly held up a sign that read: "Kennedy & Raker, Attorneys at Law." Everyone clapped.

"Now," Judge Stark said in the voice of authority that had become his trademark, "are we ready to have a wedding?"

Raker and Sarah looked at one another and then at Judge Stark, and said at the same time, with equal conviction: "We are!"

After they said their vows and exchanged rings, Judge Stark pronounced them "partners for life." Raker hesitated for a moment as he looked to Liz.

"It's OK, Daddy. You can kiss her," Liz said.

"Yes," the group shouted, "kiss her!"

And kiss her he did.

A few minutes later, as the happy couple admired their wedding rings, the best man walked up.

"They turned out pretty well, don't you think?" Edmonds asked.

"They're beautiful," Sarah said. "But how did you get the rings so quickly?"

"Santa put in a special order last night with our chief jeweler at the North Pole. He's pretty quick at his craft. Did you notice the inscription?"

Sarah took off her ring and looked inside the band. "Always believe!" she read aloud. "I will," she added solemnly.

"Me, too," Raker said. "Never again will I doubt the magic of Christmas."

Just then, Judge Stark approached with a purpose, waving a piece of paper at the newlyweds. "I still have a little clout at the courthouse, made this a rush job when you submitted your application yesterday. You two need to sign, here and here."

He handed them a pen and they signed. Afterward, he took back the pen and signed his name in a way that would have made John Hancock proud.

"You know what this does?" Judge Stark asked, in a firm, judicial tone. "It makes this entire day a legally binding Christmas. If you breach it, you'll have to deal with me and Santa Claus. He and I have discussed it. So keep it in mind."

There must have been an extra dose of magic in the room that day, because Judge Stark's eyes brightened and he began to laugh. It was the kind of laugh that put an exclamation point on an already glorious day, one that would make Santa Claus himself proud.

The End

A Note to You, the Reader, from Landis Wade

Thank you for reading *The Legally Binding Christmas*—I hope the story put you in the Christmas spirit.

If you liked this second book in the *Christmas Courtroom Adventure* series, please add a review of the book on Amazon and Goodreads. And please tell your friends. Your kind words of support will help other readers find my books.

Also, I would love to hear from you. Here are several ways we can stay in touch:

Sign up at my website: www.landiswade.com

For Facebook: www.facebook.com/thechristmasheist

Email me: landiswrites@gmail.com

Check me out on Amazon, Goodreads, Twitter and YouTube.

In the meantime, may the magic of the Christmas season lift you up each and every day. Always Believe!

Acknowledgements

A big tip of the hat to the *Christmas Courtroom Adventure* team for giving life to this story: Lystra Books & Literary Services, publisher; Susanne Discenza Frueh (Norman, Oklahoma), illustrator; Nora Gaskin Esthimer (Chapel Hill, North Carolina), editor; Karen Van Neste Owen (Richmond, Virginia), copy editor; and Beth Tashery Shannon the Frogtown Bookmaker (Georgetown, Kentucky), book designer. The wordsmiths on the team gave great advice; the fault was mine alone where I failed to choose the right words. I was confident, however, that Sue's illustrations and Tash's design would bail me out; they certainly did. It's hard to look at their work without smiling.

Hugs and kisses to my creative collaborator on the book, my wife Janet. She was my sounding board for the "what ifs." We would be riding somewhere in a car and I might say: What if there was a problem with Santa's distribution system? She might say: And what if Santa used a house in Raker's town run by elves? And I might say: What if the county exercised eminent domain to take the house? And she might say: What if Hank Snow conspired with the county? And so on, until my mind starting going in lots of directions.

Legally binding accolades to my colleague, Tommy Odom, an eminent domain attorney, who critiqued my work. Tommy tries eminent domain cases against the government on a regular basis and had some good suggestions. To the lawyers who read this book, the liberties I took with the legal process are no reflection on his skill or advice.

Hand-claps for my daughter Jordan for great feedback on the text and for helping me maintain some gender balance. "You know, Dad," she said, "the main characters don't all have to be men." That led to several changes, including a metamorphosis for Holly, the "elf-to-be." Holly started out as Bobby, a boy. Then, she was Bobbi, a tomboy girl. Then she became the elf she always wanted to be.

High-fives to my son Hamlin for modeling several positive traits that I tried to remember when I was stuck or discouraged. When he makes a commitment, he finishes what he starts, and when he takes on a challenge, he gives it all he's got.

Finally, I bow in gratitude to the readers of the first book in the series, who said, "I liked it. You should write another one." It gave me a second chance to imagine, "what if?"

Landis Wade is a civil trial lawyer, arbitrator, mediator and writer in Charlotte, N.C. He is a 1979 graduate of Davidson College, where he majored in history and played varsity football, and a 1983 graduate of Wake Forest Law School, where he was a member of the Law Review and the National Moot Court team. Landis is married, has two adult children and two rescue dogs. He enjoys sports, traveling with his family, and spending time at their cabin in Watauga County, N.C., where he likes to fly-fish, hike, bike, read and write.

Visit the author's website: www.landiswade.com

Visit the Facebook page:
www.facebook.com/thechristmasheist

Contact the author: landiswrites@gmail.com

CPSIA information can be obtained
at www.ICGtesting.com
Printed in the USA
FFOW01n0735230916
27826FF